THE MEDIC

NORCROSS SECURITY #8

ANNA HACKETT

The Medic

Published by Anna Hackett

Cover by Lana Pecherczyk

Cover image by RplusMphoto

Edits by Tanya Saari

ISBN (ebook): 978-1-922414-50-2

ISBN (paperback): 978-1-922414-51-9

WHAT READERS ARE SAYING ABOUT ANNA'S ACTION ROMANCE

Heart of Eon - Romantic Book of the Year (Ruby) winner 2020

Cyborg - PRISM Award Winner 2019

Edge of Eon and Mission: Her Protection - Romantic Book of the Year (Ruby) finalists 2019

Unfathomed and Unmapped - Romantic Book of the Year (Ruby) finalists 2018

Unexplored – Romantic Book of the Year (Ruby) Novella Winner 2017

Return to Dark Earth – One of Library Journal's Best E-Original Books for 2015 and two-time SFR Galaxy Awards winner

At Star's End – One of Library Journal's Best E-Original Romances for 2014

The Phoenix Adventures – SFR Galaxy Award Winner for Most Fun New Series and "Why Isn't This a Movie?" Series

Beneath a Trojan Moon – SFR Galaxy Award Winner and RWAus Ella Award Winner

Hell Squad – SFR Galaxy Award for best Post-Apocalypse for Readers who don't like Post-Apocalypse

"Like Indiana Jones meets Star Wars. A treasure hunt with a steamy romance." – SFF Dragon, review of *Among Galactic Ruins*

"Action, danger, aliens, romance – yup, it's another great book from Anna Hackett!" – Book Gannet Reviews, review of *Hell Squad: Marcus*

Sign up for my VIP mailing list and get your *free box set* containing three action-packed romances.

Visit here to get started: www.annahackett.com

CHAPTER ONE

She leaned against the bar and sipped her drink.

It was sparkling water in a cocktail glass. While she wouldn't have minded a real cocktail, she was working.

Siv Pedersen sipped again and glanced at her watch, then made an annoyed face.

"Nice expression," an amused male voice in her earpiece said. "It says 'that damn, good-for-nothing boyfriend of mine is late again.'"

She snorted. There was no boyfriend, she was just playing the part of an abandoned woman in a bar in order to keep an eye on her target. The guy was currently eating a filet steak medium rare at a table by the windows of the fancy steakhouse.

"He isn't worth it, Siv," the voice in her ear said. "A man should never stand up a gorgeous woman like you."

She hid her smile from the restaurant.

"Quit flirting with our newest recruit, Oliveira," came the darkly lethal tone of their boss, Vander Norcross.

"I'm a one-woman man these days," Ace Oliveira said. "I'm just making the rookie feel welcome."

Ace was also about to become a dad. He and his fiancée, Maggie, had a baby due very soon. The tech guru of Norcross Security couldn't stop sharing snaps of Maggie's very large belly.

Siv did feel welcome. She'd needed a change, and moving from Norway to San Francisco to work in private security for Norcross was proving a good decision.

Her hand tightened on her glass and she crossed her legs. After she'd left the Norwegian military, life hadn't felt right. She'd loved the Army, but she'd known it was time for a change, but civilian life had initially proved harder than she'd guessed. She hadn't found a job she enjoyed. And then once her ex, a man who professed to love her, had dumped her to marry a pretty socialite with connections, Siv had decided it was time for a change.

"Siv, target is finishing his meal." Ace's voice was all business now.

She swiveled a little and scanned the target. Mastro's Steakhouse was pretty quiet this evening, but nearby, she saw a server carrying a huge seafood platter to a table. Her gaze shifted to the man just beyond.

Anthony Patterson Robson the Third. Tony to his friends.

It was a pretentious name for a mediocre man. He was an analyst at a San Francisco tech firm, and he'd decided that making a decent paycheck for hard work was beneath him. Instead, he'd decided to try his hand at corporate espionage.

Unfortunately for Tony, Norcross provided security for his employer, Nova Tech.

"He's on the move," Ace murmured.

"Siv, are you ready?" Vander asked.

"I'm on it." She fluffed her hair. It was brown, but shot through with gold streaks. She was wearing more makeup than normal, highlighting her blue eyes.

Tony headed her way. He was good-looking enough, but boring, with a weak jaw. He reminded her a little of her ex. As Tony drew near, Siv put her plan into action.

"Damn the man." She slammed her phone onto the bar and lifted her drink. She let a few tears fill her eyes. She also let more American leak into her accent. It was easy enough. While her father was Norwegian, her mom was a California girl, through and through. Living in Norway had never softened Christie Pedersen's accent.

"Excuse me? Are you okay?"

Despite being about to meet his contact outside to hand over a flash card full of data, Tony stopped in front of her.

The man's other weakness was leggy blondes.

She shifted her legs, and watched his gaze drop. She wore a short, silver-gray skirt and a silky shirt in deep emerald green. Her hair was loose, and she tossed it back.

"I am now." She shot him a smile. "My boyfriend, make that *ex*-boyfriend, has stood me up for the last time."

Tony smiled, and flicked another glance at her legs. "I find it hard to believe that any man would stand you up."

She laughed. "I'm Eve." It made a good cover name since her real name sounded similar, just with an S.

"Eve. Look, I need to step outside and meet a business contact, but would you like to go somewhere, and have a drink?"

She pretended to consider. "You know what? Why the hell not?" She leaped off the stool and grabbed her handbag.

"Um, great." Tony's smile turned a little strained. "So I just need to hand over some files to my colleague and I'll be done."

I bet you do. She knew the man couldn't risk sharing the files on the internet, hence why he'd copied them to a flash card. She fluffed her hair again. "Sure thing. I'll touch up my makeup while you do your work thing."

Tony's smile brightened. "Great." He waved a hand toward the front of the restaurant.

She walked ahead of him and put a little extra sway into her hips. She could practically feel his gaze glued to her.

Men. So predictable.

Her ex, Johan, had been. Not at first. No, at first, he'd loved her strength. Said he was proud of her military career. Was falling in love with her.

Until he hadn't been.

She knew when it had started. A night out in Oslo with some friends. A drunk had been shouting abuse and grabbed the arm of their friend Espen's date. The woman had been scared and shaken. Siv had taken the man down in about three seconds and then passed him off to the bouncers at the nightclub.

She'd thought Johan would've been pleased. Instead, he'd been quietly furious. When they got back to his place, he'd ranted that she'd embarrassed him. He was the man, not her. He was the one who should've protected them.

Siv opened the door of Mastro's and rolled her eyes. She could open her own doors, drive her own car, lift her own bags, and defend herself. Protection wasn't what she'd wanted from Johan.

They'd broken up three weeks later, and a month after that, he'd been engaged to an elegant, well-dressed, twenty-something, whose father owned a shipping company. Siv had discovered he'd been screwing his new fiancée while he was still seeing Siv.

Siv's pride had been hurt, and she'd been mad that she hadn't realized he'd been cheating on her. It was then that she'd also, thankfully, realized that she hadn't been in love with Johan.

She'd wanted to be in love with a man who adored and respected her. But she was coming to realize that love was a stupid fairytale that the movies used to sell shit.

Total fiction.

Her parents' disastrous marriage should have already taught her that. And her father's subsequent parade of women.

Siv didn't need love. A hot night here or there would do the trick. She only needed herself—not someone who tried to erode her sense of self, her confidence, and her pride.

"I'll just be a second, gorgeous," Tony said.

"Sure thing." She pulled out her lipstick and compact from her handbag.

"Saxon is parked in a vehicle out front," Ace said. "And the contact is incoming."

She angled the compact mirror and saw a man striding up the street. Despite the warmish evening, he had a windbreaker on. The man was walking fast, like he had somewhere important to be. Some corporate espionage to conduct.

Tony straightened, looking nervous. Siv swiped some lipstick over her lips.

"Are you Mr. Black?" Tony asked the man.

"No names. You have the item?"

Tony nodded.

"Who's the woman?" the man asked.

"My plans for the next few hours."

Oh, don't you sound smug and overconfident. Siv rolled her eyes again.

For a second, another smug, overconfident male came to mind. And his outrageously handsome face and sexy smile.

No. Siv shut that down. She was not spending any time thinking about the medic who helped out Norcross Security. She wasn't spending time thinking about *any* man.

She turned and saw Tony holding out the data card.

"Actually," she said. "I'm here to take the information you stole, Tony, and stop this cozy bit of corporate espionage."

Tony frowned, looking confused.

Mr. Black was quicker on the uptake. He started to spin away, but Siv burst into action.

Her kick caught him in the gut.

The man made a pained sound and doubled over. Ooh, yes, that high heel had to have hurt.

She spun, snatched the flash card, then grabbed a still-stunned Tony's arm and yanked. She bent her legs and he sailed over her head, and fell flat on his back on the concrete.

Siv stuck the flash card in her bra. Saxon Buchanan, a blond god of a man in tailored Armani, stalked up to her.

He eyed the men. "You don't mess around."

"No," she replied.

"Nice work." He hauled Tony up. "I think we'll have a little chat with these two, then—" Saxon's eyes widened. "Siv, look out!"

There was a sudden, burning sting on the side of her rib cage. She swiveled, and saw Mr. Black, pocketknife in hand.

She kicked him, ducked another slash of the knife, then blocked his next swing.

Saxon charged into them and tackled Mr. Black to the ground, pinning the man's arms to the concrete. Siv dropped to her knees on Mr. Black's legs. The man jerked beneath them.

"*Fuck.*" Saxon lifted one hand. It was bleeding from a cut on his palm.

"He caught you?"

"Yeah." Saxon's gaze dropped and his brow creased. "But not as bad as you."

Siv looked down.

Oh, hell. Her shirt was soaked with blood.

"THERE WE GO, Bish, all good now." Ryder Morgan pressed a bandage to the now-cleaned cut on the older man's swollen foot. "You need to take your meds and keep off your feet for a while."

The homeless man nodded. His hair was tangled, and his beard was an unruly mess. He smiled, showing some missing teeth.

"Thanks, Ryder. You're the best, man."

Ryder smiled and pulled his gloves off. "Still got those shoes I gave you?"

"Uh-huh." Bish nodded, collecting his trash bags filled with his things from the corner of the clinic room.

Frustration hit Ryder's chest. He knew he couldn't save everyone who came through the doors of the Anderson Free Clinic in the Tenderloin.

The Tenderloin was fifty square blocks, wedged in between some of the wealthiest areas of San Francisco. But here, the streets were suffused with poverty. There were cheap apartment buildings and hotels, there was drug dealing out in the open, and these streets were home to more than half of the entire city's homeless.

Bish always hit Ryder hard. The man was a veteran, and had fought as a teenager in Vietnam. He'd come home, but hadn't made it through to the good life. PTSD and other mental health problems had ended with Bish living on the street.

He'd be back at the clinic in a few weeks, his feet cut up again, all exacerbated by his poorly treated diabetes, and the assholes who stole his shoes.

Bish hunted around in a bag and pulled out a pair of

Ryder's old running shoes. "Here they are." He shoved them back in the bag. "Catch ya later, Ryder."

Ryder fought back a sigh. "Yeah, man. Hey, have you seen Robbie lately?"

Bish frowned and shook his head. "Nah. Haven't seen him for a while."

Ryder hadn't either. Robbie was another vet Ryder kept tabs on. Robbie was younger than Bish, but older than Ryder. Like Ryder, Robbie had also been a combat medic and had served in the Gulf War.

When he could, Ryder bought Robbie a meal, and they traded war stories.

Unlike Bish, Robbie had a family who cared for him, and tried desperately to help him. But Robbie always ended up back on the dirty streets of the Tenderloin. Especially when the demons got too loud, and the lure of the drugs got too shiny.

Ryder sank back against the wall and closed his eyes. Yeah, he couldn't save them all, but it still fucking sucked.

Outside the treatment room, he heard the insistent wail of a crying baby, the hubbub of conversation, and someone weeping.

The clinic was always busy, and offered free medical to the disadvantaged and vulnerable of San Francisco. The Tenderloin could be tough and harsh, and Ryder did his bit to offer a little light in the darkness.

The rest of the time, he worked as a paramedic, attached to Fire Station No. 2 in Chinatown. Anyway, for tonight, his shift was almost over.

He was ready to head home, shower, jerk off, and have a glass of wine. He liked to drink a good bourbon with his brothers and friends, but Ryder's weakness was a full-bodied Napa Syrah.

One of the nurses passed by the doorway.

"Iris, I'm clocking off," he called out.

The middle-aged woman eyed him. She had a well-groomed afro, high cheekbones, and wore pink scrubs that looked good with her dark skin. "You'd better get out of here before some emergency comes through the door."

An emergency usually constituted a gunshot wound, stabbing, or an overdose.

He lifted his chin. "See you in three days."

"I will miss that fine, white ass of yours while you're gone."

He flashed her a smile. "Iris, no sexual harassment in the workplace."

She waggled her eyebrows. "You haven't seen anything yet."

He waved her off, and saw her face turn serious as she headed to intercept some parents clutching a lethargic toddler.

They all joked around. It was a way to cope with the grim reality they saw in the clinic each day.

Ryder made his way to the tiny locker room in the back beside the even tinier break room. He grabbed his backpack from his locker and decided to just wear his blue scrubs home. They weren't covered in anything hazardous today.

His cell phone rang.

Probably one of his brothers—Hunt or Camden.

He was putting his money on Cam. The youngest Morgan brother had just gotten out of the military a few months back, and was still acclimatizing to civilian life. But he seemed to be adjusting well to life in private security, and enjoyed working at Norcross Security.

Hunt was a cop, and he'd recently fallen in love with a sexy, blonde artist. He wasn't available for beers and burgers with his brothers quite as much now. Not because Savannah wouldn't let him, but mostly because he couldn't drag himself away from her.

Ryder pulled out the phone. Vander Norcross' name was on the screen.

Shit. Vander was a friend, but when he called, it usually meant someone was hurt. Ryder's third sideline job was patching up the Norcross Security guys.

"Vander."

"Hi, Ryder. I'm almost at the clinic. We need your help."

"Everyone okay?" Ryder strode through the clinic with a wave to his colleagues.

A dark-eyed girl, maybe three years old, popped up on a waiting chair and saw him. She was in cute little pink pajamas covered in polka dots, and her parents were nearby, rocking a crying baby. Ryder winked at her, and pulled a lollipop out of his pocket. He caught the father's eye. The tired man saw the candy, nodded, and gave Ryder a faint smile.

Ryder handed the lollipop to the little girl and ruffled her dark hair. She smiled at him.

"Nothing life-threatening," Vander said. "But there's a lot of blood."

Vander sounded pissed. "Cam?"

"Not Cam. He has a night off. Saxon's got a cut on his hand, but Siv copped the worst of it."

At the thought of tall, sexy Siv being hurt, Ryder's gut tightened. "How bad is she?"

"Well, she's cursing a lot in Norwegian."

Ryder hit the sidewalk out front. The night had turned a little sticky, but his thoughts all turned to Siv Pedersen.

He'd first met her at Savannah's art showing a few weeks ago. Siv was one hot, tough badass in a beautiful body. He had no problem conjuring up an image of her. Tall, toned, her military training obvious in the way she held herself.

She had a tawny mass of blonde-brown hair and blue eyes like a cloudless sky.

And a killer scowl and a smart mouth.

They'd danced, he'd tried to charm her, then she'd decked him. She'd laid him out on the dance floor with one smooth move.

Ryder wanted her. *Badly.*

He turned down a few offers of company over the last few weeks because the only woman he seemed to want was a tough, former Norwegian special forces brunette.

He'd seen her a couple times at the Norcross office, but she'd made a point to avoid him.

Ryder smirked. Well, she couldn't avoid him tonight, although he wasn't thrilled she was hurt.

A black BMW X6 pulled to a throaty halt in front of him. Ryder opened the passenger door of the SUV and saw Vander behind the wheel.

"Hey." Ryder slid in. "What happened?"

Vander pulled out onto the street. "It was a fucking simple corporate espionage job. We didn't expect the guy to pull a knife."

Vander took care of his own. He was never happy when one of his people was in danger or hurt. Most people in San Francisco went out of their way to avoid pissing off Vander Norcross.

To Ryder's intense amusement, a few months back, he'd gotten to watch Vander and Ryder's cousin Brynn do a short, intense circle around each other. It seemed that even major badasses fell in love.

Most people thought that since Vander had fallen for Brynn, it had softened him a bit. In Ryder's opinion, it made Vander more dangerous. He was intensely protective of the woman who held his heart.

Ryder hadn't ever felt the need to find "the one." Sharing his time with a variety of lovely ladies worked for him, but watching Vander's brothers, Vander, and now Hunt take the fall... Well, he was starting to wonder if they were onto something.

Then he'd taken one look at Siv Pedersen, and he needed to know how she tasted.

Well, for the moment, he was going to worry about making sure she didn't bleed to death.

CHAPTER TWO

"You don't need to fuss." Siv bit back a snarl as Saxon pressed some gauze harder to her side.

"Siv, you're bleeding everywhere. If one of your team on a mission was bleeding, what would you do?"

Get the medic to treat them. She huffed out a breath.

They were in the medical room at the Norcross Security office. Vander had converted an old warehouse for the space. The inside was a masterpiece of modern, industrial design—gleaming wood, black-metal accents, glass-walled offices.

Vander kept the medical room well-stocked. The walls were lined with shelves filled with boxes and containers of supplies.

Siv shifted on the bunk. "You're bleeding, too."

Saxon studied the bloody cloth wrapped around his hand. "Gia is going to be pissed."

Saxon was engaged to Gia Norcross, Vander's sister. The small, feisty brunette was a PR executive, and wasn't shy about sharing her feelings.

The door opened.

"Looks like you two got yourselves into some trouble, I see," a male voice drawled.

Siv's head whipped up. She worked hard to keep her face neutral and locked down her irritating response to Ryder Morgan.

"Get in here and stop this bleeding," Saxon grumbled.

Ryder sauntered in. The man didn't walk, no, he moved with this glide that instantly made a woman wonder how good he'd be in bed.

Dritt. Shit. Stop obsessing, Siv.

He set his backpack down. He was wearing blue scrubs, so she guessed he'd come from work, and they somehow looked outrageously hot on him. His thick, brown hair, not quite long enough to brush his shoulders, was tied back in a short tail.

He glanced up and green eyes met hers. They weren't dark, but were a lighter shade of green with faint flecks of gold.

He smiled at her. "You wanted my hands on you so badly that you got yourself sliced up?"

This man was the charming bad boy that every mother warned her daughter about. And cocky as hell.

"Yes, I organized the bad guy with the knife to cut me just so I could see you, Morgan." Her words dripped with sarcasm.

Her tone did nothing to dim his smile. Her best barbs seem to slide right off this man.

He grabbed some latex gloves off the shelf. "Saxon, let me see your hand."

Saxon held it out.

Siv had seen bad injuries before—in training and in combat. She didn't flinch at the sight of gore and blood.

"Wash it, then put this on." Ryder slapped a tube of something at Saxon. "After, I'll glue it, and then bandage it." He winked. "Then Gia can play nurse." Ryder turned to Siv. "Now, my lovely Norwegian flower, top off."

"I'll wash up in the kitchen." Saxon slipped out.

Siv looked at the wall. The military had cured her of any shyness about stripping and undressing in front of other people. She tried to pull her shirt up, but her side pulled. She winced.

"Hang on." He leaned closer.

She stared at a wall of hard chest. The remnants of his citrusy cologne, mixed with the scent of healthy male, hit her. Her body lit up like fireworks.

Siv gritted her teeth.

She'd come to America for a change. To leave men and the problems they caused behind. Why did her body go haywire anytime this one was close?

She would never let him know how he affected her. She knew his type: handsome, charming, used to women falling at his feet. She'd spent her formative years being raised by one, and then had dated one.

She stayed stiff as Ryder pulled her shirt off. She had to hand it to him, his touch was brisk and professional.

He gave her black bra a brief glance, then frowned at her wound. He made an unhappy sound.

"Oh, you've made a real mess of yourself."

"It was the bad guy."

"Lie back." He helped her lie on the bunk. "I hope you decked him."

"Saxon and I tackled him. Hard."

"Good." Ryder opened something, then she heard a slosh. He wiped her cut and she hissed at the sting.

"Sorry, I need to kill the germs. I'll give you something for the pain."

She grunted.

He swiftly cleaned it and made a sympathetic sound.

Siv glanced at his face. Damn him for being so gorgeous. Not in a pretty way. No, Ryder Morgan was all man: rugged with a sexy edge.

"I'm going to glue most of it, but one cut will need a couple of stitches," he told her.

She nodded.

"It'll leave a bit of a scar, but I'll make my stitches as neat as I can."

She shrugged. "I have other scars."

His green gaze flicked up to hers. "Me, too."

She rolled her eyes. "You sound proud."

"I can show you, if you think I'm lying. We can compare."

Traitorous heat coiled in her belly as she imagined seeing every inch of his hard body. Damn this out-of-control desire. "I'm good." She looked at the ceiling.

Ryder got to work. He gave her painkillers and swiped something on her skin to numb the area.

Saxon reappeared and Ryder dealt with gluing the man's hand.

"I'm heading home," Saxon said. "Thanks for the help tonight, Siv."

"Thanks, Saxon. I hope Gia doesn't give you too much of a hard time."

The man smiled—slow and sexy. "She will. Then she'll feel a strong need to take care of me."

A swift pang of...something hit Siv. It was clear the handsome man adored his fiancée. And when she got back to her new, almost-empty apartment, there wouldn't be anyone who felt a need to take care of her.

"See you tomorrow," Saxon said. "Take it easy, Siv." The door closed behind him.

"Right, let's get you fixed up." Ryder dragged a stool over.

Siv stared at the ceiling as he got to work. He was gentle. It surprised her. She'd pegged him as an arrogant charmer, but Vander was no one's fool, and he clearly trusted this man with his people's health and well-being.

"Okay?" Ryder asked.

She nodded. Her fingers curled into her palms. She was so damn aware of him.

She couldn't resist looking down. His big hands moved gently over her skin. The man knew what he was doing.

He had tattoos on one arm, and her gaze traced the black ink covering his strong forearm. She saw overlapping scales and swirls. It looked like it was part of a dragon.

She looked at the blue fabric of his scrubs and wondered what the rest of the tattoo looked like.

"I wish I'd seen it," he said.

She blinked. "What?"

"I wish I'd seen you in action." He grinned. "There's

nothing sexier than watching a badass woman take a bad guy down."

She stared at him. Was he serious?

He pressed a bandage to her side. "Keep it dry. I'll check on it tomorrow." He gave it a little pat, causing sensation to skate through her body.

She nodded and sat up.

His gaze dropped, and his smile widened.

"I like your skirt." Then he spun around and reached over to a shelf and pulled off a plain, black T-shirt. "Your pretty, green shirt is ruined, I'm afraid."

She pulled the large T-shirt on. *Why did this man affect her so much?* She'd been well known for her cool control on her FSK team. The Forsvarets Spesialkommando were the best special forces unit in the Norwegian Armed Forces.

She'd dated Johan for a year and had never felt this driving need to get her hands on him. Ryder confused her. She'd thought she had him pegged, but he kept surprising her. His competent, professional demeanor clashed with her idea of the cocky playboy.

"You did well, Siv." He pulled a lollipop from his pocket and handed it to her. "Now, I'm going to drop you home, and maybe you can try and stay out of knife fights for a day or two."

"I'll try," she replied dryly.

She took the candy. What she really needed to do was to stay away from Ryder Morgan.

THE NEXT DAY, Ryder finished restocking the back of the ambulance. His shift was almost over, and they'd had a hell of a day. A fire, several car accidents, two overdoses, and a heart attack. He rubbed the back of his neck. They'd lost a young woman at one of the car accidents. He blew out a breath.

He knew he couldn't save every patient, but that didn't mean it didn't hurt.

"Morgan."

He looked up. "Sir?"

Captain Shane Ferguson was a neat, trim, fit man who wore his uniform well and ran Fire Station No. 2 with a firm hand. "I wanted a chat."

"Sure thing. This rig is clean and restocked." Ryder leaped out and closed the back doors. "What did you need, Captain?"

"I want to try and convince you to take a full-time paramedic position. You're damn good, and we need the help."

The captain tried a few times a month to get Ryder to go full-time.

"Part-time suits me." When Ryder had first gotten out of the Air Force, it had taken a while to readjust. The pressure of full-time hadn't been what he'd needed then.

Now he was busy, between paramedic shifts, working at the clinic, and helping at Norcross Security. A part of him liked giving back at the free clinic.

Easton Norcross, Vander's older brother, was a savvy billionaire businessman. He'd helped all of them invest their money. Early on, Ryder had saved all his money while he'd been in the military. Being on active duty, he hadn't needed much.

Now, he owned a place in Chinatown that had six apartments and a couple of shops downstairs. One apartment was his, and if he wanted to, he could live quite happily on the rental incomes and still cover the mortgage.

But healing, helping someone who was hurt or injured, was in his blood. He couldn't not be a medic.

"I like the work I do at the clinic in the Tenderloin, Captain. Those people need help, too."

Captain Ferguson released a breath. "Understood. And it's hard to argue with that." He cupped Ryder's shoulder. "If that ever changes, you just need to let me know."

"Thanks, Captain."

Ryder finished up and clocked off, then headed over to his motorcycle.

The Triumph Street Triple was mostly black, with touches of red on it. It was fast, agile, and had a little touch of attitude that he liked.

He pulled out his cell phone and found the number he wanted. The call connected.

"Why is your number programmed in my phone?" a clipped, female voice said.

God, he loved that snotty tone. "Because I put it there."

"How did you get *into* my phone?" Siv demanded.

"Trade secret. How's the side?"

"Fine."

"Siv, no lollipops for ladies who lie."

She huffed out a breath. "It stings."

"Any redness?"

"A little."

"I want to take a look." He threw his leg over his bike. "You at the Norcross office?"

"No. I was meeting an informant in Chinatown."

"That's where I am." After he checked on Siv, he planned to try and track down Robbie. "Can you meet me at the clinic in the Tenderloin?" He gave her the address.

A pause. "Fine."

Hmm, it probably meant that her cut was hurting more than she was sharing. "You take your pain pills?"

Another pause. "Not today. They make my head foggy."

"Take the pills, Siv."

"I'll see you at the clinic." She hung up.

Buoyed by the thought of seeing his prickly Norwegian, Ryder gunned the bike and headed toward the clinic.

The bustling maze of streets and alleys, full of dim sum joints, restaurants, souvenir shops, bars, and herbalists, gave way to the grittier chaos of the Tenderloin.

Even though he spent a lot of time here, he never got used to the trash, tents, and debris littering the sidewalks. People lingered on street corners, and drugs and money visibly changed hands.

As he rode, he kept an eye out for Robbie, passing a few of the man's favorite haunts. There was no sign of him.

Ryder pulled up in front of the clinic and pulled his helmet off.

A couple of kids loitering by the corner raced over.

"Hey, Doc," a skinny, white kid called Joey said. The pre-teen had a mop of dark curls.

His best friend Caleb, shorter, with dark skin and a shaved head, followed behind. "Yo, Ryder."

"Hey, guys. Joey, I'm a medic, remember, not a doctor."

The boy shrugged a shoulder. "You're always in those blue doctor outfits, and you've got a scope thingy."

"Today I'm in this uniform." He pointed to his shirt. "Paramedic."

Caleb cocked his head. "I think I could be a paramedic."

"Do it." Ryder offered his fist and the kid bumped it. "It's a good job."

"Too much blood and puke for me." Joey sniffed. "I'm gonna be a badass, like your friend, Norcross."

Ryder grinned. "Then you have some work to do."

Joey straightened. "We'll watch your bike for you. Five bucks."

The boy regularly extorted Ryder to keep an eye on the Triumph.

"I won't be here long." He saw a black X6 pull up. "Two-fifty."

"Shit. Three."

"Deal."

Siv stepped out of the vehicle. She wore bootleg-cut, dark jeans, a white shirt, and a brown belt. Her hair was up in a ponytail.

"Holy sweet legs," Caleb muttered.

Joey spotted her and gave a low whistle.

"That one's all mine," Ryder told them quietly.

"You lucky bastard," Joey muttered.

"You guys are way too young, anyway."

"One day I won't be." Joey puffed up his chest. "Then I'm gonna find myself a looker with long legs."

"Amen," Caleb said.

Siv stalked over. "Morgan." Her blue gaze flicked to the boys. "These your friends?"

"Yeah, Joey and Caleb, this is Siv."

"Seeve." Caleb rolled her name around.

"You're a looker," Joey announced.

Her lips twitched. "Thanks."

"Hey, have you guys seen Robbie around?" Ryder asked them.

Both boys shook their heads.

Fuck. He was getting worried.

"Last time I saw him, he was eating at Dan's Kitchen, with some fancy dude in a suit," Joey said.

Dan's was a favorite diner in the area, done in retro-style. Hmm, the guy in the suit might have been Robbie's brother. Ryder might need to ask Vander to track down the brother's number. Maybe Robbie was staying with his family for a while.

"Okay, watch the bike." Ryder jerked his head to Siv.

They walked into the clinic. It was a one-story, unassuming building done in a plain beige. The clinic ran on donations and there wasn't much in the budget for making the place pretty.

Pushing through the front door, he held it open for

Siv and scanned the waiting room. It wasn't too busy, with just a few people seated in the plastic chairs. An older black woman was sitting down, flanked by worried-looking family. Another man looked pale and sweaty. He was maybe in his late twenties and didn't look too good. He hunched over, staring at the floor.

Ryder glanced at the reception desk and spotted a familiar face.

"Hey, Santiago, you got a spare room I can use for a minute?" Ryder asked.

Santiago was a short, lean, handsome Hispanic man and experienced nurse. He lifted a hand to Ryder and glanced at Siv. "Ryder, this ain't a hotel, and if it only takes a minute, she needs to trade you in."

Siv snorted.

Ryder rolled his eyes and grinned. "I need to check her wound."

Santiago smiled. "Go on. Exam Five is free."

"Thanks, man. Hey, have you seen Robbie lately?"

Santiago frowned. "No. Not for a while. The last time he was in, he was flush with cash. Said he had some side job."

Ryder raised his brows. "He never mentioned a job to me."

"If I see him, I'll let him know you're looking for him. Maybe ask Jacko. I think he treated Robbie."

"Okay, thanks."

Ryder showed Siv into the exam room. It was plain, with grubby, beige walls and a stained, linoleum floor, but it was clean and serviceable.

"Who's Robbie?" she asked.

Ryder waved at the bunk. "A friend. He lives on the street, and has a drug problem, but he's in good health. He's a veteran. I keep tabs on him."

She jumped up on the bunk, and he felt her staring at him.

He looked up from a tray of medical equipment. "What?"

"I'm just trying to work you out."

He held out his hands. "What you see is what you get, my lovely Siv."

"No. Men think they're simple, but they're not. They have no clue what they want."

There was a faint bitterness to her voice and Ryder paused. "Did some man break your heart? Want me to beat him up for you?"

CHAPTER THREE

Siv looked at her hands, then back up at the big, handsome male in front of her.

Seeing another side of him today got her mind churning. The sexy, dangerous-looking motorcycle definitely fit with her image of Ryder as the womanizing bad boy. But the dark-blue paramedic uniform, and joking around with kids on the street, and concern for a homeless veteran...

Damn Ryder Morgan for not fitting in the box where she wanted to shove him.

"No broken heart," she said. "That was part of the problem. He maybe bruised my pride a little bit, but my heart barely felt it."

Ryder pulled some latex gloves on. "He why you left Norway?"

She moved a restless shoulder. "He was part of it. I left the military and tried a few different jobs, but hadn't found my groove. Then I discovered the man who said he loved me was sleeping with a newer, sweeter model. I needed a change."

Ryder lifted her shirt, then peeled the bandage off. "Well, I'm glad you picked San Francisco, Siv."

"Ryder, I'm not interested in flirting, dating, or a charming man."

He cocked his head. "How about hot sex?"

She choked back a laugh. "You are relentless."

"I have two brothers, so I've learned to be persistent."

"I'm not against hot sex." Sex with Johan had been good. Maybe not exactly earthshattering, but good. "But not right now, not while I'm starting a new job and taking a break from men."

"Are girls okay then?" He waggled his eyebrows.

She huffed out a laugh, then he touched her side and she hissed.

"You need to take the damn pain pills, Siv. You have some infection trying to settle in. I'll organize a prescription for an antibiotic."

"Fine."

He cleaned her injury and re-bandaged it.

She pulled her shirt down and sat up. He ripped his gloves off.

"Where's my lollipop?" she asked.

He grinned and tucked her hair behind her ear. He made a lollipop appear from behind it.

"Oh, look."

She shook her head and took the candy.

Then he gripped her chin, his gaze hot.

She froze and her insides went haywire. *Dritt.* She

couldn't let him see how much he affected her. She was done handing men any power over her.

Her heart wasn't broken, but she still had a few dings. Some from long before Johan.

And a man like Ryder Morgan would enjoy her for a bit before moving onto the next pretty, young thing who caught his eye. She'd seen the women around here. The men at Norcross all had excellent taste when it came to their partners. Gia, Harlow, Haven, and hell, even a princess, were all gorgeous. Yes, Maggie was a helicopter pilot and Vander's woman Brynn was a cop, but they all still had far softer edges than Siv.

"Back off, Morgan."

"You change your mind on the hot sex thing, you let me know."

"If you don't want me to deck you again, back off."

He held her gaze, then stepped back.

Siv leaped off the bunk. It was time to get away from Ryder Morgan and clear her head.

He led her out of the exam room. "I'll call you again tomorrow."

She made a sound.

His brows drew together. "If it gets worse, you call me."

"It'll be fine."

A young man in scrubs stepped out of a room. He was far shorter than Ryder but had broad shoulders. Tattoos wound around both his muscular arms and his head was shaved.

"Jacko," Ryder said.

The man lifted his chin. "Hey, Ryder." He shot Siv an appreciative grin.

"Siv, this is Jacko. Jacko, my friend, Siv."

Siv nodded at the man.

"Have you seen Robbie?" Ryder asked. "I haven't seen him around."

Jacko frowned. "Haven't seen him for a few weeks. Sorry, man."

Ryder released a breath. "Okay. Thanks. If you see him, tell him that I'm looking for him?"

"Sure thing." A pained groan echoed from a nearby exam room. "I'd better get back to it."

Siv followed Ryder into the waiting room. A pale man staggered up out of his chair, shaking and sweating profusely.

She frowned. "Hey, are you all right?"

The man stumbled into her.

Dritt. She caught him before he crashed to the floor.

Ryder spun, cursing. He helped her lower the guy to the floor.

"Santiago, code red," Ryder yelled.

They crouched, just as the man started convulsing.

"Jesus, what's wrong with him?" Siv asked.

Ryder didn't reply. He was too busy checking the man's vitals and loosening his shirt. Ryder had gone totally into the zone and was completely focused on the sick man.

"Shit, he's crashing," Ryder yelled. "Santiago!"

Ryder started chest compressions. Siv sat back, feeling helpless.

Suddenly, the clinic staff raced in. Ryder barked

medical terms at them, and soon they were lifting the man onto a gurney and wheeling him out.

"*Fuck.*" Ryder scraped a hand through his hair. His hair tie had come loose, and his brown hair fell around his handsome face.

She suddenly realized how tired he looked. He'd worked a paramedic shift, then checked on her, and now this.

Santiago appeared, face grim. "Looks like full organ failure."

"What?" Ryder said. "How do you know?"

"The second one we've had this week." Santiago shook his head and cursed. "I know this guy. Angelo. We saw him three weeks ago and he was perfectly fine. For someone living on the street, he was in good health."

"It can't be organ failure," Ryder said.

"Last one was the same. Just crashed. No prior health issues."

Ryder frowned, staring at the door where they'd taken Angelo. "Drugs? Maybe he took something?"

"Maybe." Santiago pulled in a breath. "I'd better go check. See you later, Ryder."

When Siv and Ryder stepped outside, it was much warmer, but she still felt chilled. She wondered if that poor man would make it.

"Are you okay?" she asked.

Ryder released a breath. "Yeah. It's just been a long day. I'm going to go home and have a drink. Tomorrow's a new day."

She wondered if it was really that easy for him to switch off.

He shot her a charming smile. "Can I get a kiss goodbye?"

"No."

"A hug?"

"No."

He leaned close and she saw the flecks of gold in his eyes. Damn him for being so tempting.

"What are you so afraid of, Siv?"

That I'll fall for you, and you'll hurt me. She didn't know where the internal voice came from, but it made her hunch her shoulders. "I'm not afraid, I'm just not interested."

He grinned. "Liar."

"Go home, Morgan." She headed for her SUV. "And deflate that big head of yours."

"If I'm lucky, I'll dream of you."

She unwrapped her lollipop, then licked it before sucking it into her mouth.

He groaned. "Evil woman."

She swirled her tongue around the sweet.

He gave a longer groan. "You're killing me."

"Sweet dreams, Morgan."

She was smiling as she climbed into the BMW. She loved the Norcross SUVs. As she pulled out, she saw Ryder slipping money to the kids watching his bike.

But his gaze was on her vehicle. Making sure she got away safely.

Yes, Ryder Morgan had dangerous complications written all over him.

Complications she didn't need or want, and that her bruised heart wasn't willing to risk.

IN THE KITCHEN at the Norcross office, Siv filled her coffee mug. *Mmm.* The scent tickled her nostrils. She was enjoying all the different coffees and variations that her new country offered.

This morning, she'd spent time with their tech guru Ace, learning some surveillance ropes. Her side throbbed, but it was bearable.

She'd woken a few times during the night, mostly because she'd rolled onto her wound. And once or twice she'd woken because she'd been dreaming of a green-eyed medic.

Quickly, she sipped her coffee and burned her tongue. She cursed in Norwegian.

Cam strolled past. "That sounds nice, but I bet it isn't."

She jerked her chin, thinking how much he looked like his brother. A more intense version, with shorter hair, and a scar on his cheek. What he'd been through in the military was still stamped all over him. Even she'd heard about the extraordinary exploits of the mysterious Ghost Ops teams of the American military. They were the best of the best.

"If my mother heard me, she'd give me a lecture," Siv said.

"Yeah, moms, you can't escape the mom glare. Mine has it down to a fine art."

Siv sipped her coffee. "You're close with your mother?"

"Yeah, dad died a few years back. The three of us

keep an eye on her. She's tough. Had to be since she was a cop's wife, and mother of three boys who all joined the military."

Mrs. Morgan must be made of titanium.

"She's pretty happy now that Hunt's loved up with Savannah." Cam frowned. "God, I hope she doesn't start pestering me and Ryder to settle down."

"Your brother doesn't strike me as the settling-down type."

"He just hasn't found the right one. Ryder's got a big heart, but he hides it with a smart mouth. How about you? Are you close to your parents?"

"I'm close to my mother. Both she and my father live in Norway. They've been divorced for years. I rarely see my father. He sends me a birthday card each year."

Cam nodded.

"Usually it's a month late and written by one of his assistants. He's had two wives since my mother, both progressively younger."

"Ah," Cam said.

"My mom is American, but fell in love with Norway. She loves the winter. She calls me every few days and despairs that I've moved to another country." Siv sipped her coffee. "And wants me to not get mixed up with any slick, American men." Or any man like her father.

Down the hall, Vander and his woman, Brynn, appeared. They lived in a large, loft apartment upstairs above the office. The detective wore a blue shirt tucked into navy-blue pants, accented by a brown belt with her handgun and police badge clipped to it. Her brown hair was in a braid, and she looked like a woman more than capable of defending herself.

She said something to Vander, who gave the woman a smile. Siv blinked. She didn't see her boss smile much. He hauled Brynn in for a kiss that was neither short nor polite.

Siv looked away.

"Those two do that all the time." Cam shook his head. "Never expected Vander to fall in love, and definitely not with my cousin."

"Siv?"

Turning, Siv saw the couple headed toward her. Brynn smiled and lifted a hand.

"How are you settling in? These guys aren't driving you crazy yet."

Vander tugged on Brynn's braid.

"So far, so good," Siv said. "I'm really enjoying the job."

"That's great," Brynn said. "Look, I need to get to the station, but let's grab a beer some time."

"Sounds great."

"I want to help ease you in before Gia or Harlow finally kidnaps you for a ladies cocktail night."

"Oh?" Siv had never really had time for nights out with girlfriends.

"They'll grill you on everything, and get up in your business." Brynn shook her head. "They mean well, but you've been warned. They're already plotting who to hook Cam up with."

Cam made an annoyed sound.

"Right, I'm out of here." Brynn went up on her toes and kissed Vander's jaw. "Catch you later, Norcross."

The detective strode out.

"Hey, Siv." Ace popped his head out of his office. "I have more to show you."

"On my way." She nodded at Cam and Vander.

She spent the next few hours trying to memorize everything Ace was showing her.

Finally, tech man stood. "That's it for now. I've got to meet my baby mama for lunch."

"Thanks, Ace. I'm going to go over some of this a bit more."

"I'll quiz you when I get back." He winked on his way out.

Siv's cell phone rang and she saw it was her mom. She did a quick calculation and realized her mom had probably just finished dinner and would be curled up in her Oslo apartment with a mug of warm cider.

With a smile, she answered. "Hi, Mamma."

"There's my girl. How are you, darling?" Christie Pedersen sounded like she'd lived in California her entire life, although she spoke excellent Norwegian. She'd been a flight attendant when she'd met Siv's father.

"I'm good. Busy with the new job."

"You like it. I can tell."

"I do."

Her mom let out a gusty sigh. "I miss you, but I'm glad, my darling. I am certainly happy you're rid of that slick, slimy Johan."

"Mamma—"

"I'm just staying it how it is."

Siv sank back in her chair. "I was the one who missed the signs."

"That he's *exactly* like your father." There was venom in her voice, old and faded, but there. "Charming, always got excuses, worried about putting on a show for the 'right' people." She sniffed. "He never appreciated you."

"I know, Mamma. I told you, he hurt me, but he didn't break my heart."

"You steer clear of men, Siv. They aren't worth it."

It hurt Siv that her mom had never let go of her heartbreak over Henrik Pedersen.

"It's okay, I have no plans to get involved with anyone." A handsome face with green eyes popped into her head, but she squelched it. "I'm making do by enjoying looking at all my new work colleagues. They are *så kjekk* and wear a suit so well."

Her mom made a sound. "I don't care how handsome they are—"

"They're also mostly happily in love or engaged."

"Good." Her mom's voice softened. "I miss you, darling, but I'm glad you're happy and finding your feet."

"Me too."

"I'm proud of you."

Those words warmed Siv's heart. "Don't make me cry, Mamma."

"I wish your father would tell you that," her mom added sourly.

Siv looked blindly at Ace's wall of screens. Her father had always told Siv that she was not feminine enough, not graceful enough, not sweet enough. He'd never come to any of her sports games at school. When she'd joined the military, he'd been extremely disapproving.

Since she barely saw him, she'd never let his thoughts worry her too much.

"Mamma—"

"I know, I know." Her mom paused. "I just wish Inger was here. So I could see both my girls as beautiful, accomplished women."

Siv pressed her lips together. It had been two decades since her little sister had died, but Siv often thought of that smiling, blonde fairy. She wished she could remember Inger's voice, but it was too long ago. "Me too, Mamma."

"I didn't mean to make you sad. Now, I'll let you get back to work."

"Okay. Love you."

"Love you too, darling."

Siv ended the call, then turned back to the computer screens.

"Siv?" Vander appeared in the doorway. "My office."

"Sure thing."

In Vander's spacious office at the end of the hall was a dark-haired, middle-aged man in a suit. Siv summed him up with a glance: well-off, designer suit and watch, contained, composed face. She guessed he was a successful businessman.

"Siv, this is Peter Wilcox. Peter, this is one of my employees, Siv Pedersen."

She nodded. The man rose and held out a hand.

He looked hollow, tired, and tense, like he was holding back emotion. Thanks to the military, she was pretty good at reading people. She'd been through a number of training courses, and specialized in hostage situations, so she had the skills to read a person quickly.

"It's nice to meet you, Ms. Pedersen."

"Siv is fine."

He took his chair again, while Siv slid her hands into the pockets of her suit pants.

"Peter's brother died," Vander said. "He wants us to look into it."

"Okay," she said. "You haven't had any luck with the police?"

Peter shifted in his chair. "The medical examiner ruled that my brother's death was due to living on the street and his drug addiction."

"I'm sorry."

"He was in the Army, and when he came home, he had trouble settling. His demons haunted him, along with a healthy dose of PTSD. His mental health declined."

Siv thought of the people Ryder dealt with in the Tenderloin.

Peter gripped the back of his neck. "I loved my brother. We all tried, time and again, to help him, but he always ended back up on the streets."

"He used drugs?" Vander asked.

"Yes. Thomas dabbled, but he wasn't a hard-core addict. Sometimes, he wanted to dull the demons." Peter shook his head. "I idolized him when we were kids. He was friendly, athletic, always smiling. But after the Army... He was never the same."

"Siv and I are both former military, Peter," Vander said. "We understand."

Peter nodded. "Thomas was in excellent health. I had lunch with him every week. Ensured he had everything he needed." Peter sighed. "Or at least what he'd take from me."

Siv's chest tightened. How horrible to love someone, but be helpless to help them.

"The last time I saw him, he was happy. He said he was doing some odd jobs, feeling good. He was as fit as a horse, and he bragged about his daily sit-ups and push-ups." A faint smile crossed Peter's face. "It was why he never let his addiction go too far. He liked being fit."

"How did he die?" Siv asked softly.

Peter ran his hands through his hair, mussing it. "He missed our standing lunch date. I searched for him, but there was no sign of him. It wasn't uncommon. I just hoped he was busy." Peter pulled in a shaky breath.

"But he wasn't." Sympathy for the man flooded her.

"No. A few days later, his body was found behind a dumpster at the edge of the Tenderloin and the Theater District. I thought maybe he'd been attacked or overdosed."

"That wasn't what happened?" Vander asked.

"No. I identified his body. There wasn't a mark on him. The medical examiner said there were no illicit drugs in his system at the time of his death, but his long-term drug use must've contributed to his organs failing. It's bullshit. He was healthy."

"The medical examiner didn't say anything else?" Vander asked with a frown.

"No. He rushed me out of there. I have some connections, so pulled in some favors. I got a copy of Thomas' autopsy. He died from complete organ failure."

Siv frowned, a chill running through her. "Caused by what?"

"They blamed his drug use. There's no damn way that's what killed him. I don't have rose-colored glasses on about my brother and his problems, but I'm convinced someone stole his life from him. After everything he'd been through—" Peter shook his head violently "—he didn't deserve this. I want justice for my brother, Vander."

Siv saw the glint in Vander's eyes. There was no way her boss would let this slide.

"Send through the autopsy report. I'm putting Siv on the case."

She nodded. "I'll find out who killed your brother."

Relief flooded Peter's face and he stood. "Thank you."

Vander saw the man out, then returned.

"You need anything, you let me know," Vander said.

She nodded. "He didn't deserve this."

"No, he didn't. We need some medical knowledge to understand what exactly happened."

She stiffened. She suspected she knew where this was headed.

"I want you to connect with Ryder. Go over the autopsy report together."

Hell. She'd been afraid he was going to say that.

She pasted on a smile. "Sure thing."

She'd do her damn job, and resist the charms of a certain medic.

CHAPTER FOUR

Pushing through the doors to Norcross Security, Ryder smiled to himself. He was excited to see Siv. Even excited for her to nip at him.

He liked her bite.

Vander had also left a message that he needed a medical consult on a case. It wasn't often, but Vander sometimes pulled Ryder in on certain cases.

Saxon stepped out of an office and waved his bandaged hand. His jacket was off, but he looked flashy in his suit pants and gray shirt. Ryder had the day off, so he was just in jeans and a black T-shirt.

"How's the hand?"

"Healing up nicely." A pleased smile crossed Saxon's face. "Gia decided I can't do anything at home. So, she's doing all the cooking, and in bed, I get to lie back and enjoy the show."

"Lucky bastard."

Siv appeared at the end of the hall. She was talking with Vander's younger brother Rhys. She was in slim, gray pants and a black shirt, and Ryder's cock throbbed. Damn, she was something.

"That one won't let you sit back and enjoy the ride," Saxon said dryly.

Ryder grinned. "Nope." With Siv, it would be a hot, sexy battle.

"If she ever lets you close enough to touch her...in a non-medical way."

"I'm not a rich boy like you, but I am charming."

Siv strode their way, and when she spied Ryder, a scowl settled on her face.

Saxon snorted. "Yeah, good luck."

"My side's much better today," she said.

"Hello to you, too. It doesn't matter, I still need to look at it." Ryder smiled. "How's my lovely Norwegian flower today?"

Her eyes narrowed. "Don't push it, Morgan."

He took half a step closer. "I can't help it. Whenever I look at you, I'm overcome."

"I can help you get over that."

"Really?"

When she stepped closer, he smelled fresh soap. He liked that. No flowery scents for Siv.

Her face softened, her gaze on his lips. "Yes, I can."

He breathed her in, his gaze dropping to her mouth. Her lips were full and sexy, and gave him all sorts of ideas. All he could think about was Siv.

Her fist landed in his gut, driving the air out of him.

Ryder bent over.

Siv smiled. "See. Now you're thinking of something else."

He huffed out a laugh. *Fuck.* It was probably best not to tell her that he was hard. Just the thought of tussling with her turned him on.

"Come on." She nodded toward the medical room. "Let's get checking my cut out of the way, then I'll give you a rundown on this case. It concerns a homeless veteran. I know you keep tabs on a few of them."

He nodded. Again, he worried about Robbie. The man still hadn't checked in.

In the medical room, Siv unbuttoned her shirt and slipped it off.

Ryder froze.

Her black bra was mostly sheer, with just a touch of lace at the edge. He could see her nipples clearly.

Shit. He bet she'd done this on purpose to torment him.

He swallowed. He took his job seriously. He was attracted to Siv, but he would never make her feel uncomfortable in this room.

She sat on the bunk, watching him steadily.

"You wore that on purpose." He pulled on some gloves. Crap. His hands weren't exactly steady.

"You don't factor into my underwear choice, Morgan."

He bent over to remove the bandage. Her wound looked much better today. He quickly treated it and re-bandaged it.

"It's looking good. You're taking the antibiotics?"

She nodded.

He shifted, and found his face way too close to that gossamer bra cupping her firm breasts lovingly. He swallowed a groan. Then he turned, stripping the gloves off and discreetly adjusting his aching erection.

When he'd found a shred of control, he turned.

Siv had her shirt back on, thank God.

"You done torturing me?" he asked.

Her lips quirked. "Maybe." Her face turned serious. "Now we need to go over my new case."

The seriousness in her tone made him nod. "Lead the way, my Norwegian snow flower."

She made a choked sound. "Snow flower?"

"I can totally see your beauty thriving in the snow. Toughness beating the cold."

She rolled her eyes and stalked out.

Ryder smiled. This was the most fun he'd had in... well, ever. He followed her out and saw Rome Nash striding down the hall.

"Hey, Rome."

"Ryder." The big bodyguard wore a dark suit and a white shirt. He kept his dark hair cut short, and his green eyes were sharp and alert.

"How's Sofie?" Ryder asked.

Rome scowled. "Good. I'm going to meet her now. She has a photo shoot."

Princess Sofia of Caldova supported a lot of charities, and did a lot of interviews and photo shoots.

"Why the scowl?" Ryder asked.

"It's a *naked* photo shoot," Rome grumbled.

"Ah." Sofie was classy and royalty, and she knew her overprotective fiancé very well. "I'm sure she won't bare too much."

Rome straightened. "Hell yeah, because I'll make sure of it." With a wave, the big man strode off.

Vander stepped out of the conference room and jerked his head.

"What's this case you need help with?" Ryder asked. He spotted Siv leaning against the wall, a file in her hand.

"A family wants us to investigate the death of their brother," Vander said. "He was a vet, with PTSD and other mental health issues. He didn't settle back into regular life. Ended up dabbling with drugs and living on the streets."

Ryder shoved his hands in his pockets. A story he saw way too often. "I deal with people like that all the time at the clinic. They can't cope with regular life, even with a loving, supportive family behind them. Most of them don't even have that, though."

Vander took a seat, and Ryder did, too.

"Siv's the lead on this case," Vander said.

"Was the guy murdered?" Ryder asked.

"We need to work that out," Siv said. "The brother insisted that despite some drug use, his brother was healthy and fit."

Ryder nodded. "It's survival of the fittest on the street. People prey on the weak. Some of the guys do what they can to stay as healthy as possible."

"His brother's body was found with complete organ failure," Siv said.

Ryder frowned. Alarm bells started ringing in his head.

"What?" Vander said, eyeing him carefully.

"We've had a few cases through the clinic lately.

People off the streets we know, who are generally in good health. They've come in with organ failure."

Siv dropped into a seat beside him. "That man in the waiting room at the clinic...?"

Ryder nodded. "He didn't make it. According to my colleagues at the clinic, he'd been fine just a few weeks ago."

Vander sat back. "Poison? A new drug?"

"Maybe."

"The medical examiner wasn't interested," Siv said. "They blew off our client and said that his brother's drug use was to blame, even though he didn't OD."

"I heard at the station that there have been problems at the Medical Examiner's office." Ryder frowned. "Don't remember the details, but they lost their accreditation last year."

"That could have contributed to them blowing off Peter," Vander said.

"Or no one really cares about a dead, homeless guy," Ryder added. It was a sad reality he'd seen before.

Siv set the file down. "Can you take a look at the autopsy report?"

"Sure." Ryder flipped the file open. "I'll just—" The world spun sideways.

He stared at the name on the file, then the washed-out picture of the corpse with gray skin.

"Ryder?" Siv frowned.

He stood abruptly, and his chair tipped over. "Thomas Wilcox."

Her brow creased. "Yes, our client Peter's brother."

"That's Robbie." Sorrow crashed into Ryder.

"Thomas Robert Wilcox." Ryder closed his eyes. "He's dead."

THE ANGUISH on Ryder's face cut through Siv.

She'd lost teammates in the military. One good friend, Rolf, had saved her life once. She bit her lip. He'd fallen from an oil rig platform during a hostage situation. She hadn't been able to save him.

She saw the same grief on Ryder's face that she'd felt when Rolf had died.

"Ryder." Vander stepped forward.

Ryder made an enraged sound, then turned and punched the wall. His fist went through the drywall.

Then he pressed his hands to the back of his neck. "Fuck!" He kicked a chair and sent it toppling.

Vander stepped forward, but Siv held up a hand.

"I've got this," she murmured.

Vander eyed her for a second, then nodded. He stepped out of the room, closing the door behind him.

Siv moved closer to Ryder. She felt the pain throbbing off him.

"Hey." She reached out, her fingers brushing his back. His muscles were so tense under the well-washed, cotton T-shirt.

"He didn't deserve this." Ryder's voice was a low growl. "He didn't always have his shit together, but he was a good man."

"I know."

Ryder spun and grabbed her hand, his eyes angry.

"Robbie fought for his country. He had a damn medal for risking his life to save the lives of other soldiers. On the street, he looked out for others and kept the predators away. He was one of the good guys."

"I'm so sorry, Ryder. I know it hurts."

"*Fuck.*" He reeled her in.

She didn't fight it. Hell, she didn't want to. A part of her wanted to help him with his pain.

When he wrapped his arms around her, she leaned into him and pressed her face to his chest.

She heard the rapid beat of his heart, and unsurprisingly, felt hard muscle under his shirt. He hadn't gone soft since he'd returned to civilian life.

Siv slid her arms around him. "Just hold on."

He let out a shuddering breath and pressed his face to her hair. "He could've been me."

She frowned. "What do you mean?"

"Robbie was a combat medic. Patching people up in a war zone, you see some messed-up shit. Horrible, horrible injuries. People in agony. People crying for their loved ones. People who die in your arms." His body shuddered. "It's hard to deal with all that. You come home and everyone around you is normal. They watch TV, they head to the grocery store, they bitch about their bosses and work. They get mad over stupid shit, not knowing, not comprehending what others sacrifice for them."

"I know." She hugged him tighter.

"I could have been Robbie. When I came home, it took me weeks to settle down. I couldn't sleep, couldn't acclimatize. Nothing felt right. Hell, I slept on the floor most nights because the bed was too soft."

"You made it," she said quietly.

"Yeah. My mom and Hunt, my friends... They were there until things evened out. But I was close to being Robbie, and walking away."

"Robbie's death is not your fault, Ryder."

He ran his hands up her back. "I always feel like I should do more for them, that it's never enough." He let out a long breath. "I've mostly learned to deal with it."

He stepped back.

She studied his handsome, serious face.

"It's *not* your fault," she said again. "Now, do you want to help me find out what happened to him?"

There was a flare in Ryder's green eyes. "Yes."

"Let's go over that autopsy report. Can you handle that?"

Ryder nodded. Then he reached out and stroked her cheekbone.

She felt that small touch burn through her, and locked her knees. She wasn't going there. She couldn't let him see how much he affected her.

Especially now. This was her first case with Norcross, and she wanted to do a good job. She needed a clear head and Ryder's help to do that.

She sat back at the conference table. Ryder dragged in a deep breath, dropped into the chair beside her, and picked up the file.

Siv watched the focused way he read the report. Her gaze fell to his hands. He had nice ones: strong, long fingers, competent. Hands that could heal or protect.

She crossed her legs. *Jeez, Siv.* She was sitting there obsessing over a man's hands.

He flipped the page. "Toxicology shows some odd results. He had elevated THC levels."

"Marijuana?"

Ryder nodded. "Robbie used weed when things were getting a little bumpy. To take the edge off. He turned to the harder stuff when the demons got bad." A groove appeared in Ryder's brow. "But there are some other spikes in here."

She leaned forward. "A different drug?"

"Yeah. But the ME said the levels weren't high enough to cause his death."

"Robbie didn't mention trying anything else?"

Ryder shook his head. "Robbie wasn't the kind to try the new, designer stuff."

"And the other people in your clinic who died of organ failure?"

Ryder sat back in his chair. "I need to get their autopsy reports."

"Maybe someone is cooking up a new drug on the streets."

"Maybe, but I know Robbie—" Ryder paused "—I *knew* Robbie." Ryder looked down and his hand on the table turned to a fist. "He wouldn't take a new drug."

Before she could stop herself, she reached out and wrapped her hand around his fist.

His fingers loosened and entwined with hers. "Like I said, Robbie never took anything crazy. He knew it could be laced with crap. He wouldn't have done it."

"Okay."

"You believe me?"

She nodded. "You might annoy me most of the time, Morgan, but I believe you."

His fingers stroked her wrist and she pulled her hand away, afraid he'd realize her pulse was racing.

"So, we need to check on the other people who died at the clinic." She tapped a finger against her lip. "And check with hospitals and other clinics, because there could be more."

"Maybe this is an allergic reaction to something." His mind ticked over. "We need to question Robbie's friends on the street. They might know something."

"Give me a list and I'll track them down."

His green gaze locked on her. "They'll never talk to you."

"I can make them talk."

"It'll be easier if I'm with you."

Her stomach swirled, like a bunch of insects taking flight. *Work with him? Side-by-side?* "I can handle this."

"He's right." Vander's deep voice from the doorway.

They both swiveled.

Her boss eyed Ryder. "You got a lock on it?"

Ryder nodded. "I want to help catch whoever killed Robbie."

His voice was firm, determined.

"I can put in for some time off," he added.

Oh, no. "This is *my* case. I've got this."

Vander nodded. "I know, but you need to utilize all your resources, Siv. We need Ryder's medical knowledge and his contacts on the street."

Dritt. She folded her arms. "So what, I'm the muscle?"

"No, you're the lead," Vander said. "Find Robbie Wilcox's killer for our client. And do it with Ryder's help."

Dammit. Now she was officially working with Ryder Morgan.

CHAPTER FIVE

Ryder sat in the passenger seat of the X6 while Siv drove.

His mind was still churning.

Robbie was dead. *Fuck it all.* He knew better than to get too close to the people he took care of at the clinic. The streets were a tough, unsafe place to be, but he couldn't help it. Especially not with the veterans.

Not when it cut so close to home.

"We'll head to a few places that Robbie hung out," Ryder said. "Track down his closest friends."

She nodded and turned a corner. Unsurprisingly, she drove well, despite being new to the city. She had steady hands and didn't get flustered. That seemed to apply to everything Siv did.

And hell if it wasn't damned attractive.

At first, it had been her looks and confidence that had drawn him, but he was learning that there was a lot more to like about Siv Pedersen. Like the way she'd held him when he'd lost it over Robbie.

Tough and soft. A deadly combination wrapped up in a sexy body.

For a second, his brain conjured an image of her naked, under him, taking his cock.

Shit. He shifted to ease the pressure. Now was not the time.

"Ace is already working on finding similar cases at other clinics," she said.

Ryder nodded. "I'll make some calls as well, and talk to my colleagues." His hand curled. Whoever the hell was responsible would pay. He'd make sure of it.

He gave Siv directions and she found a parking space near the first of Robbie's hangouts.

They climbed out of the SUV. "I know you're a badass, but stay close and do your best to avoid a confrontation."

"I'm not a total newbie, Morgan," she said.

"I know." They headed down the cracked sidewalk.

There were tents ahead, lined up along a chain-link fence. Ryder stepped over a pile of trash and used needles. He clocked two guys with heavy ink standing in a shadowed doorway. They watched Ryder and Siv pass by with hard eyes.

"There's an alley up here," Ryder said. "Some of the homeless congregate there." He turned into it.

The ripe stench of rotting trash and excrement hit them. He saw Siv wrinkle her nose, but that was it.

She'd probably been in some equally hellish places before.

Toward the back of the alley, beyond some large dumpsters, he saw several people huddled together.

Some had tents set up, while others had canvas sheets and tarpaulins strung up as makeshift shelters.

The people all froze, eyeing Ryder and Siv with suspicion as they approached.

Ryder spotted a familiar face. "Hey, Bish. You all right?"

"Oh, hey, Ryder." The older man limped over.

"Feet okay?" Ryder asked.

Bish shrugged, stroking his scraggly beard. "I still have two of them."

But he wouldn't if he didn't take better care of his diabetes. "You taking those meds I gave you?"

"Sure, sure." Bish sniffed and eyed Siv. "This your woman?"

Siv opened her mouth.

"Yeah." Ryder slid an arm around her, ignoring her stiff body.

"You sure know how to show a girl a good time, Ryder. Should take her to a fancy restaurant or somethin', not this fine establishment." Bish cackled.

Ryder smiled. "She knows I'll treat her right." Their gazes met for a humming second, before he looked back at Bish. "Bish, I need to ask about Robbie."

"That old coot must've hit a good thing, 'cause he ain't been around." There was a flash of quickly hidden hurt on Bish's face. "He's normally not gone this long."

Fuck. Ryder closed his eyes for a second. "Bish, Robbie's dead."

The older man's mouth opened, closed. He gave a strained laugh. "No way. Robbie's too tough to croak. He even says that, that he's like old boot leather."

Ryder let out a breath. "His body was found in an alley off Eddy Street. I'm trying to find out what happened to him."

The color drained from Bish's weathered face. "Not Robbie." The man swayed.

Siv beat Ryder, grabbing the older man's arm. She helped him over to a dirty, rolled out sleeping bag. She didn't hesitate to help Bish, despite his less-than-pleasant odor.

"Sit down," she murmured. "Take it easy."

"Robbie... Aw, hell." Bish's voice cracked. "He was the best of us. He helped so many people."

Ryder crouched in front of Bish. "He had some side job. You know what it was? Who he was working for?"

Bish shook his head. "He had some cash. He gave me some when I needed food. He helped out some others, too."

Of course, he had. That was typical Robbie.

"He said it was a good gig. Easy money."

Ryder frowned. *Doing what?* He had to find out. "But you don't know where, or who was paying him?"

Bish shook his head.

Damn. Ryder met Siv's gaze. His frustration was echoed in her blue eyes.

"Wait." Bish snapped his fingers. "He said Scratch was doing it with him."

"Scratch?" Siv asked.

"Another vet," Ryder said. "Young. He's only been out a couple years. He lost some fingers in Afghanistan in an IED blast. He has some anger management and anxiety issues, and couldn't keep down a job. He beat a guy up in a bar fight, then ended up on the street."

Bish nodded. "Scratch might know." Then the man's shoulders sagged. "Poor Robbie." Tears welled and Bish swiped his forearm across his face.

Ryder gripped the man's shoulder. "He'll be missed. But we'll remember him."

"Why Robbie? What the hell happened?" Bish looked bewildered.

Ryder squeezed again. "I'm going to find out, I promise. If someone is to blame, I'll make sure we get justice for Robbie."

Bish nodded. "Um, will there be a funeral or something? I'd like to pay my respects?"

"I'll find out from Robbie's family. They want to know what happened to him."

"He said they were good people." Bish sniffed. "They never gave up on him."

"I'll let you know, Bish." Ryder rose. "You hear anything, come to the clinic and let me know."

Ryder and Siv left the alley. He flexed his hands.

A deep anger was welling inside, tapping into deep reservoirs he kept well hidden. Ones where he'd stored all his past rage at what he'd seen, done, and coped with in the military.

Where the sorrow for the lives he hadn't saved brewed and festered.

He took a deep breath. He thought all those feelings were gone, but he realized that they were just laying low and simmering.

"You all right?" Siv asked.

She was watching him like a bomb about to detonate.

"Not really."

That's when he saw three men heading down the sidewalk toward them.

They were all wearing jeans and stained T-shirts. One was heavily inked, while another was completely bald. The third man had shaggy, dark hair.

They were all big and broad, and their gazes were locked on Ryder and Siv.

"Trouble at twelve o'clock," he murmured.

Siv shifted slightly, fiddling with her ponytail. She was good. She didn't tense up or give away that she was looking at the men. Her gaze skated over them in a millisecond.

Then she looked back at Ryder, and hell, she had an excited glint in her eyes.

"You know how to fight, medicine man?"

He snorted.

She smiled. "I think we can handle this."

And he was getting hard just imagining her taking care of things.

Now was *not* the time.

He loosened his shoulders as the gangbangers got closer. The one with the bald head looked jumpy, eyes bright. He was high on something.

Ryder narrowed his gaze.

This was just what he needed to dispel the tension riding him hard. He flexed his hands.

Bring it.

SIV TURNED and eyed the men. One was tall, with a shaved head, and his gut straining his T-shirt. Another one had tattoos up his arm and neck, and was shorter, but muscular. The last guy wasn't big or small, and had a lot of shaggy hair.

They all looked mean.

"*Chica*, I like the look of you." Tattoo Guy grabbed his crotch, his gaze running over her.

Siv kept her face blank. "Sorry, Romeo, I can't say the same about you."

Shaggy Hair snickered, while Tattoo Guy scowled.

"I'm gonna mess up your pretty boy," he spat.

"Pretty boy?" She raised a brow at Ryder. "Is he talking about you?"

Ryder shrugged a shoulder. If he was worried about the threat, he didn't look it. "Can't be," he said. "I'm handsome, rugged, and chiseled."

She snorted. "And modest."

"Come on, you know you agree."

She shook her head. "How do you walk around with that big head of yours?"

"*Hey*." Shaved Head looked confused and annoyed.

"Sorry, you three are used to people being frightened and intimidated, right?" Siv made a face. "I could try."

Ryder nodded. "Let's see."

She kept her face blank and voice monotone. "Oh, please don't hurt us."

He shook his head sadly. "That's lame."

She shrugged. "I'm just not feeling it."

"Bitch, we're gonna mess you and your pretty boy up," Shaggy Hair spat.

"And *chica*," Tattoo Guy drawled. "I'm gonna have a little fun with that smart mouth of yours." He rubbed himself. "I bet you love sucking cock."

Siv rolled her eyes. "Actually, I do."

Beside her, Ryder groaned. "No sucking cock talk right now, please."

She couldn't stop a grin. "But I don't like doing it with guys of dubious hygiene, and the way you keep scratching your crotch, you might want to get yourself checked."

Their three accosters stared blankly for a second.

Then Tattoo Guy's face twisted. He charged.

Siv lunged, swiveled, and elbowed the man in the face. His head snapped back. She landed a kick to his side, then punched him.

He let out a long groan.

She followed with two more quick jabs. Tattoo Guy collapsed in an ungainly pile on the concrete.

She straightened and stretched her neck.

Shaved Head bellowed, and he and his friend charged.

Ryder lunged in and attacked Shaved Head.

Siv had half a second to appreciate the fact that Ryder Morgan could totally fight, before Shaggy Hair attacked.

Her blood fizzed. She couldn't deny that she liked a good, physical fight.

It got the blood pumping.

Shaggy Hair swung a fist and Siv ducked the man's arm. She rammed her knee up into his gut.

He grunted and staggered back.

She smiled. "We having fun yet?" Her chop hit him in the throat, and he gagged and doubled over.

She flicked out her leg and caught his ankle. Her tug knocked his feet out from under him.

He hit the ground on his front and tried to get up, but she went down on one knee and landed another chop to his back.

He slumped.

She rose and saw Ryder watching her.

She stiffened. This was the moment when she'd see vague horror and discomfort on his face. The worry that maybe she could take him, emasculate him.

He stood with a boot on the back of a groaning Shaved Head. It looked like he'd had no trouble taking the guy down. He wasn't even breathing heavily.

Ryder's gaze met hers. He grinned, a distinctly heated look in his eyes.

Her heart thumped in her chest.

"That—" Ryder jerked his head at the man on the ground "—was hot."

Who was this man? He was looking at her with a mixture of pride and lust on his face.

She pushed her own desire back and crouched. She took a handful of Shaggy's hair and lifted his head up.

His face was already swelling a little, and he groaned.

"Who sent you?"

"Fuck... You."

"No, that's not going to happen." She yanked on his hair until he yelped. "Who sent you?"

"Some guy offered us money to mess with anyone

who came around asking questions about the dead, homeless guy."

She shook him. "What guy offered you money?"

"Dunno," he bit out. "Just a guy. In jeans. But he had really shiny teeth."

So not another person off the street. *Hmm.*

She rose. "If I cross paths with you again, I won't take it so easy on you."

The guy made a gurgling sound.

Leaving the three men where they lay, she and Ryder headed back toward the SUV. She glanced ahead. They were right on the edge of Chinatown, and she saw red-colored signs for restaurants and red lanterns strung across the street.

"Who do you think sent them?" she asked.

"Someone with secrets they don't want uncovered."

There was darkness in his voice.

The heat of the fight was wearing off, and Siv saw the anger and sorrow were creeping back in. Ryder's broad shoulders were tense, his mouth a flat line.

She hated how much this got to him. He gave so much of himself to the people he took care of.

"Want a drink?"

He glanced sideways at her.

She looked down the street. "You know a good bar around here?"

"Yeah." A muscle ticked in his jaw.

They walked side-by-side a few blocks, and he led her to a small dive bar. A neon Budweiser sign blinked in the window.

They stepped through the door. Inside was nothing

special. It was an ordinary, slightly seedy bar with red-painted walls, and a display of bottles behind a scarred, wooden bar.

The place was mostly empty, with a few patrons nursing their beers at booths at the far end.

Ryder and Siv snagged two stools at the bar.

"What do you want?" she asked him.

"Tequila."

She raised a brow. "Roger that."

She nodded at the pretty, curvy bartender. "A bottle of tequila and two shot glasses."

The woman's eyes widened, and she pushed a dark curl off her face. She glanced at Ryder with blatant appreciation, before reaching for the tequila.

Soon, the woman set the bottle and glasses down in front of them. Siv poured two shots and held a glass to Ryder.

"To Robbie," she said.

He took it. "To Robbie."

They knocked them back.

The alcohol burned a pleasant path down her throat.

Ryder slammed his glass down. "Again."

Siv poured.

They shot again. *Phew*. It packed a punch.

Then Ryder set his glass down, reached out and dragged Siv's stool closer to his. Their legs bumped and her pulse spiked.

"Morgan—"

"I know something that will hit the spot better than tequila, and leave less of a headache tomorrow."

Damn that low, sexy voice of his. It was tempting, but

she knew she should push away. But the dark emotion lurking in his eyes got to her.

And the insane urge to soothe him.

She gripped the front of his T-shirt, yanked him close, and kissed him.

CHAPTER SIX

Fuck. *Fuck*. She tasted better than anything.

Ryder opened his mouth and took the kiss deeper. There was so much simmering inside him, but it all went quiet, leaving just his desire for this woman.

He slid a hand into her hair, hauling that delicious mouth closer. He made a hungry sound.

She bit his bottom lip hard enough to sting. Yeah, that was his tough, hot, warrior goddess. She came with a delicious edge.

Her breasts pressed against his chest. Ryder wanted her naked. He wanted his hands all over that smooth skin. He wanted to hear the sounds she made when she came.

Then she pulled back, panting.

"Come home with me." His voice was gritty with need.

She let out a breath. "No."

"Siv—"

"You're angry and upset."

"That doesn't change the fact that I want you." He poured another shot.

"I get wanting some oblivion, but I'm not some pill to take to forget the shit for a few hours."

He knocked back the tequila and savored it. "You know it's more than that."

She crossed her arms. "Well, I value both of us more. If the situations were reversed..."

Fuck. He wouldn't want their first time to be when she was sick with grief and angry for justice.

He growled and poured another shot.

She touched his wrist. "Go easy, yeah?"

"I don't want easy." He shrugged her hand off. "You don't have to stay."

"Ryder..." She blew out a breath and stared. "You're actually growing on me, despite my ban on men. I'm attracted to you."

Heat coiled in his gut.

"But I was burned by an asshole recently. I'm going slowly this time. Now, I'm visiting the ladies room. If you want to get smashed, go ahead. I'll make sure you get home."

He watched her cross the bar, long legs and fine ass encased in those sleek, gray pants.

"I wouldn't turn you down."

He turned his head. The pretty brunette bartender with all the curves leaned on the bar. She made sure he got an excellent eyeful of her cleavage.

God, she was probably early twenties. Too young for him.

Hell, every woman seemed too young now, compared to a tough-as-nails, ex-Norwegian special forces soldier.

"Thanks, sweetheart."

She pulled a pen out of her pocket and grabbed his arm. She scrawled some numbers on his skin. "I'd be happy to help you fuck your troubles away."

Just a few weeks ago, he would've considered the offer.

Now, he'd let her down easy. He touched her hair. "That's a mighty tempting offer, but no thanks."

The woman leaned closer, her lips a whisper from his. "I bet I taste sweeter than her and could bounce on your cock better."

Ryder felt a flush of heat. He wasn't dead. He smiled. "Thanks again, sweetheart, I—"

He sensed a presence behind him and looked over his shoulder.

Siv's gaze dropped to where he touched the woman's hair, then the phone number on his arm, then back to his eyes.

He watched her face shut down, like a layer of slow-moving ice coating her.

"Looks like you've made plans." Her voice was like a blade. "You can find your own way home."

"Siv—" Ryder rose. His senses were already a little dulled from the tequila.

She held out a hand. "You're your own man, Ryder. You can fuck whoever you want, it just won't be me." She flicked her gaze past him. "I've no interest in joining your harem."

He growled, lunged, and caught her hand. "I don't have a damn harem."

"You're a player," she hissed. "All men are."

"I'm not your fucking ex."

She stepped in, then wrenched his arm up behind his back.

"*Fuck.*" Pain shot through his shoulder.

She shoved him forward, and when he caught himself, she was striding out the door.

Dammit. Ryder jogged after her. "Siv!"

"Just go back inside, Ryder. Drink the tequila, fuck the bartender."

With a growl, he caught an arm around her waist. He narrowly avoided an elbow to his cheek.

"Let me go!"

"No." He lifted her off her feet. "You're going to listen to me."

She was strong, but he held her. Then he spun and pinned her to the wall of the bar.

He saw the flash of surprise on her face.

"I'm trained, too, Siv. And I'm stronger than you." Their faces were inches apart. "I'm not some player. I'm not your ex. Am I a single guy who enjoys mutual, no-strings-attached sex occasionally? Yeah."

"I don't care!"

"Fuck, you're stubborn."

She tried to get free. They scuffled, but he kept her pinned.

She sagged against him with a huff, then let loose with a string of Norwegian he was sure he didn't want translated.

"Siv—"

"*Faen.*" She leaned up and kissed him.

His brain short-circuited. All he could do, all he wanted to do, was feel. Their tongues dueled. It was an angry kiss, with tongues and teeth. She got a hand loose, and he half expected a punch.

Instead, she slid a hand into his hair. She ground that long, lean body against his.

God, his desire was hotter than fire and it had claws.

Suddenly, she shoved him back.

She stood there, licking her lips. He knew she was trying to piece her armor back together.

"Siv—"

"No." She held up a hand. "Just don't."

Frustration boiled over inside him. "Stop being so damn independent and stubborn. You softened when my mouth was on yours."

Frost hit her eyes. "Johan used to say something similar. I was only soft in bed."

Dammit. "I'm *not* him."

"Go back inside, Ryder." She broke free and stalked off.

For a second, Ryder thought about going after her, but he knew they'd fight. She needed time to cool down.

He watched her stiff back as she disappeared and pressed a hand to the back of his neck. He closed his eyes. He'd messed that up. Siv Pedersen was tough, but she had a soft underbelly she tried to hide.

He looked at the neon bar sign and thought of Robbie —dead and gone.

Screw it. Ryder had a bottle of tequila at home.

He'd pay for their shots, then go home and get drunk in peace.

AT FIRST, Ryder thought the thumping was in his head.

With a groan, he opened his eyes.

He was sprawled diagonally on his bed, naked, with a tequila-induced headache. It was pounding happily behind his eyes.

"Shit." He rolled and heard the thudding again.

Someone was pounding on his front door. He sat up.

The room whirled a little, and he heard a hiss. His cat, Crank, lifted his head and glared at Ryder with one yellow eye. Crank was a stray that Ryder had befriended near the clinic, and finally adopted. He had a long, rangy body, gray fur, and the temperament of a rabid pack of wolves.

The asshole had scratched Ryder up a few times, and believed that Ryder's apartment was his own domain. Ryder just existed to open cans of food.

"Screw you, Crank. I'm not the one banging on the door." Ryder grabbed his boxer shorts off the floor, yanked them on, and strode out. He checked the peephole and saw Cam's face.

Shit. He was supposed to meet his brother for breakfast. He pulled the door open. "Sorry. I slept in."

Camden stepped inside. He was ready for work at Norcross, in a tailored, blue suit. The sleek clothes contrasted with his short hair and scarred face.

Cam did a visual sweep of Ryder's apartment—the

living area and kitchen weren't huge, but they were perfect for Ryder. A huge TV was attached to the wall with a state-of-the-art sound system, a large bay window let in lots of light, and the honey-colored wooden floors were nice. There wasn't much decoration except for a gray rug and slightly wilted plant that his mother had bought him. Crank loved to scratch up the rug and occasionally puke on it.

Ryder's brother still had that battle readiness and situational awareness from active combat. Ryder knew Hunt was worried about Cam, but Ryder trusted that Cam would relax in time. He'd adjust.

Unlike Robbie.

"You mean you went on a bender," Cam said.

Ryder closed the door. "Siv snitched."

"She was worried about you. Said you were in some bar, doing shots and flirting with the bartender."

"The bartender was flirting with me. And I came home, very alone, and did my shots here." He waved to the coffee table and a half empty bottle of tequila on it. "I have a headache to prove it." He sighed. "My friend Robbie is dead."

"The former combat medic. Siv mentioned. I'm sorry, Ryder."

Ryder ran a hand over his hair. "Yeah. Looks like someone killed him."

"Siv seems highly competent. She'll work out what happened."

"Oh, she is that and more." Ryder eyed Cam. "And she's mine." With two brothers, he knew it paid to stake your claim early.

That got him a half smile from Cam. "Does she know that?"

"Yes."

Cam's green eyes narrowed. "Is Siv on board with that?"

"It's a work in progress." Ryder smelled bacon and his gaze dropped to the brown paper bag in his brother's hand. "Tell me you brought breakfast."

"Yeah. I figure the first priority was ensuring you were alive, then feed you."

"I fucking love you, bro." Ryder reached for the bag.

Crank sauntered out of the bedroom, tail swishing. The cat hated everyone, but for some reason, loved Cam. He rubbed against Cam's legs.

"That is still the ugliest cat I've ever seen," Cam grunted.

Ryder pulled out a bacon and egg sandwich and tore into it.

"He doesn't care if he's ugly. We all have a few dings." Ryder pointed to the jagged scar on his bare chest.

Cam frowned and touched the scar on his cheek. A bomb had exploded very close to Cam and his team. Cam had lost some guys and had been injured. "Yeah, a few of us more than others." He took the second sandwich out of the bag.

Ryder dropped onto his navy-blue couch and bit into the bacony goodness. *Mmm.* Just what he needed.

"Siv didn't seem happy with you, bro, even if she was worried about you." Cam sat beside him.

"I'm growing on her."

Cam grunted and bit into his sandwich.

"I did mess up with her. She's skittish because of an asshole ex who was a player. She saw that woman flirting with me and wasn't happy."

"And you do like to flirt."

"I'm open and friendly, not a blank-faced, grouchy asshole. You should try it sometime." Ryder eyed Cam. "How are you doing?"

"Don't start. Hunt's always prodding. Mom's always turning up at my place with home-cooked meals because she was 'in the neighborhood.'"

Ryder frowned. "She never drops food off to me."

"Because she's not mother-henning you."

"She's a mom. It's in her DNA to worry. You just got home, so she's making sure you're really okay." Ryder paused. "Are you okay?"

Cam growled. "I'm fine."

"Have you gotten laid yet?"

Another growl "Butt out, asshole."

"I'll take that as a no. You'd be more mellow if you had."

Cam took another bite of his sandwich, then passed a bit of bacon off to Crank. The cat ate it, then stared balefully at Ryder.

Clearly, everyone was pissed at him today.

"So, I need to work with Siv today on this case," Ryder said.

"I am sorry about your friend Robbie, Ryder."

"Yeah." Sorrow was a punch to Ryder's chest. "I want to get her something. A little apology."

"To worm your way back into her good books?"

"Exactly. So, what have you noticed that she likes?"

Cam tilted his head. "Putting a bullet between a bad guy's eyes?"

Ryder rolled his eyes. "Um, something else, maybe."

Cam nodded. "We sometimes get a delivery from this bakery—"

"You do? I've never seen this."

"The goods go fast. They have some awesome stuff. There's this Nutella-stuffed cookie thing..." Cam moaned.

"What does this have to do with Siv?"

"She's fast. As soon as the delivery comes, she always grabs one of the buns. It has blueberries, and some sort of cream cheese frosting."

"Hmm. What bakery?"

"Flour and Branch."

Ryder ate the last of his bacon and egg sandwich. *Excellent.* He had a plan now. "Thanks, Cam."

"It's your turn to buy breakfast next time."

"Deal. And Cam, if you ever want to blow off steam, have a few too many drinks, or grab a movie, let me know."

Cam looked at him for a beat. "Yeah. Thanks, Ryder."

Ryder rose. "Now, I need to shower and head out to meet my Norwegian flower."

His brother raised a brow. "You call her that to her face?"

"Yes."

"And you're still breathing? A miracle."

"She punched me once."

Cam laughed. "Fuck, it sounds like you liked it."

"I like her." Ryder shrugged a shoulder. "She's tough. She's real. And she hides it, but she cares."

"She knows what you've been through. She gets it. Unlike the pretty things you flirt with."

Ryder rubbed the back of his neck. "Yeah."

"Well, good luck, Ryder. I'd expect a few more punches, if I were you."

Ryder saw his brother out, then grabbed his phone.

He dashed off a text to Siv to meet him in the Tenderloin to track down Scratch.

Right. Shower, dress, then a quick visit to the bakery.

CHAPTER SEVEN

Siv leaned against the SUV, watching people pass by.

She'd visited some bad places, all across the world. Every city had their dirty, gritty areas full of suffering, but she didn't think she'd ever get used to it. She watched some people shuffling into a cheap, single-room-occupancy hotel across the street. She'd learned that these types of hotels were common in the Tenderloin, and provided cheap housing for people who had nowhere else to go.

She blew out a breath. She'd lost it with Ryder the night before. He wasn't hers, and she had no say over what he did. Or who he did.

An oily taste coated her mouth as she pictured that pretty, lush bartender coming on to him.

Siv was mad at herself. He'd been upset, hurting, and she'd lost her temper with him.

She blew out another breath. She hated not being in control. She hated feeling all churned up like this.

Some girls walked past. They were young, barely in

their teens, but wearing tight dresses and too much makeup. They shot her curious looks before joining some dangerous-looking boys at the end of the street.

She needed to focus on her case. To find Robbie's killer, they needed to find Scratch. She'd smooth things over with Ryder, then keep things professional. Get the job done.

That's when she saw Ryder striding down the sidewalk. Her heart did a little pitty-pat. *Dammit.*

He was in well-worn, dark jeans, and a gray T-shirt that lovingly hugged his firm chest. The sleeves cut into his muscular biceps, and she clocked that interesting tattoo wrapped around one of his arms. The overlapping scales and other flourishes were a piece of art.

His green gaze locked on her and he gave her a small smile.

She felt it in her belly. Damn, why did her body react so strongly to this man?

"Hey." He stopped in front of her.

"Hey." She pulled in a breath. "Look—"

"Siv—"

They both spoke at once.

His smile widened. "Ladies first."

"Look, I had no right to get mad at you last night. I just wanted to clear the air."

He held his hands behind his back, his gaze on her face. "Siv, I know I said some things that triggered you, and that woman at the bar—"

"Is none of my business."

He stepped closer and his cologne hit her. A hint of lime, sharp and sexy, just like him.

"It's totally your business since we're going to be a couple."

Her thoughts scattered. "What?"

"You and me." That dangerous smile curled his lips. He whipped a hand up.

He was holding a clear container and inside was a bun. It looked like the blueberry ones from Flour and Branch.

It was her favorite. She'd developed a thing for them.

He held it out. "My apology. *Unnskyld.*"

He mangled the Norwegian word for sorry. "We *aren't* a couple. We're working together."

"Uh-huh." He lifted the dessert.

"Ryder, listen to me. I'm not getting involved with any man."

He opened the box and pressed the pretty little treat into her hand.

"We're already involved," he insisted.

She cursed under her breath. "You're so stubborn, Morgan. I think your head is harder than a block of ice."

He smiled. "Eat your bun. Then we'll go and find Scratch."

Well, she couldn't let a delicious bun with cream cheese frosting go to waste. She took a big bite.

He watched her, with way too much satisfaction on his face.

Flavor exploded in her mouth. *Mmm,* so good. She swallowed. "This doesn't mean anything, Morgan."

"Sure, it does. By the way, I looked up some other Norwegian words."

She raised a brow.

"*Faen*. You used that last night. Naughty, naughty."

"I bet you say fuck all the time."

"*Dritt*. That one rhymes with the English version." His smile was wide. "*Helvete*. Hell. I like that one."

"You actually pronounced that well."

He gave a little bow. "Next up, I'm learning some endearments, so stay tuned."

She shook her head.

"Now finish up. We're going to head to Hot Zone."

"What's that?" she asked.

"A popular gathering spot for the homeless. A bit of a tent community."

Once she'd finished the bun, they headed down the street. Tents lined the sidewalk, and the stench of urine was overpowering. Trash was littered in piles and she saw numerous discarded needles.

"It's sad," she said.

"It is." He slid his hands into his pockets. "A complex situation with no easy solution. People like to think if you just did *this* or the politician just did *that*, it would magically solve everything. But if you actually spend time here, live here, or work here, you know it's not that easy."

She glanced his way. "It gets to you."

"Of course, it does. All I can do is help as many people as I can at the clinic. And remind myself that I can't save all of them."

They reached the Hot Zone. The tent encampment was on a wider section of sidewalk, with a few trees running down the center. The tents were a multitude of bright colors, but it didn't add any cheer to the place.

As she looked around, Siv watched drugs change

hands. Small groups of older people, most with unkempt clothing, huddled together. Younger ones with woolen hats pulled low, despite the warm day, talked in low voices. One man had cardboard tied to his feet as makeshift shoes.

She saw a couple of teenaged kids, too. Far too young to be out alone. They stuck together, their watchful gazes scanning their surroundings.

"There's Nico," Ryder said. "He sometimes hangs with Scratch. Let's see if he knows where he is."

Siv stayed quiet and let Ryder take the lead. She got endless suspicious looks, but everyone seemed to like Ryder. He got smiles, and even some flirtation from an ancient woman with no teeth. He flirted back. The man just couldn't help himself. She realized now the flirtation was built into his DNA.

But the man was smart and a good paramedic, and she knew he could be serious, as well.

A realization hit her as she watched him. He also used the charming demeanor like a shield. She cocked her head and watched him. A shield to not let people too close, or let the situation get to him too much.

He glanced at her. "What?"

"Nothing."

"Most people haven't seen Scratch for a while."

She really hoped Scratch hadn't also died in some back alley.

"Backdoor Bob said he saw him earlier today. Scratch was acting weird, in a rush. He was over near the clinic."

She raised a brow. "Backdoor Bob?"

Ryder grinned. "It isn't dirty. He collects doors."

She blinked. "Right."

They headed out of the Hot Zone. Ryder led them to another street, packed with tents and makeshift shelters. There was a small gathering of people, many spaced out and high. A few were leaning against a wall, barely conscious.

Face grim, Ryder crouched and checked several of them, pressing his fingers to their wrists. "Pulse rates are steady enough."

"They're all high as kites."

Ryder knelt in front of a woman. "Angel, it's Ryder."

The blonde woman blinked. It was impossible to tell her age. She could have been anywhere from twenty to sixty.

"Have you seen Scratch?" he asked.

The woman blinked slowly, smiled. She was really out of it.

"Yes." Angel giggled. "Right behind you."

There was no one behind Ryder. Siv sighed.

But Ryder glanced back over his shoulder. A man had just appeared at the end of the camp, walking quickly, with agitated movements.

Ryder rose.

The man was thin, with baggy jeans hanging off his lean hips. His dirty-blond hair stuck out from under a ball cap, and he had a scraggly, thin beard. He looked like he was in his twenties.

The man saw Ryder, and his face drained of color. He turned and took off at a half run, half walk.

"Scratch?" Siv asked.

"Yes," Ryder replied.

They broke into a run, and so did Scratch. The man moved fast, like a frightened rabbit. He darted down the sidewalk, and when he reached a chain-link fence, he scrambled over it like a monkey.

"Shit," Ryder bit out.

Siv picked up speed. She gripped the fence, climbed, then swung herself over the top.

She landed on the other side, right in front of Scratch.

The man's nondescript, brown eyes widened. She gripped the front of his shirt and slammed him against the fence.

"I didn't do nothing!" He was sweating.

Ryder climbed the fence—all strength and easy moves. He dropped down beside her.

"We aren't going to hurt you," he said.

Scratch blinked. "Oh, ah, Ryder. Hey." The man wouldn't meet Ryder's gaze. "Tell her to let me go."

Ryder nodded and Siv released Scratch.

The man straightened his flannel shirt.

"You okay, Scratch?" Ryder asked.

The guy was pale and sweating hard. He ran a hand under his nose. "Yeah. Been sick, but feeling better now."

Ryder frowned. "You need to go to the clinic. Get checked over."

"Yeah, yeah, maybe I will." He was nervous, shifting his feet.

"I heard that you and Robbie were working a job."

Scratch froze, his face stricken.

Ryder sighed. "You know Robbie is dead."

"Oh, God." Scratch looked at his scarred boots. "Yeah, yeah. Poor Robbie."

"Who hurt him, Scratch? Who did this?"

Scratch pressed his hands to his face. "Poor Robbie. This wasn't supposed to happen."

"Tell me," Ryder insisted.

Scratch shook his head wildly. "I can't say. I don't want to die."

Siv watched. The man was terrified.

Ryder grabbed Scratch's arm. "Let me help you."

"No one can. Those people—"

Siv straightened. Ryder did, too.

"What people?" Siv asked.

Scratch made a sound. "Can't say anything. They'll kill me." He pushed away from Ryder.

"Scratch—" Ryder sidestepped.

"I gotta go." The man paused. "You'll...take care of Robbie?"

Ryder sighed. "Yes."

"Good. Good." Scratch's shoulders sagged.

"Go to the clinic, Scratch. Get checked out."

"Okay." His voice was in the silent whisper. "Trelaskin."

Then he ran.

Siv frowned. "Trelaskin? What does that mean?"

"I've no idea." Ryder's jaw tightened. "But we're going to find out."

RYDER DRUMMED his fingers on the dash as they drove back to the Norcross office.

"Stop that," Siv said.

He stopped the tapping. "Sorry. I'm thinking."

"Whoever or whatever this Trelaskin is, Ace will find it."

"Yeah."

She turned and merged into traffic. "How come you don't mind me driving? My ex was always fighting me for the driver's seat."

"Your ex sounds like an asshole prick."

"No arguments there." She dragged in a breath. "I think the problem was that I was in the military when we met. We never lived together, just saw each other on R&R. And not really that often."

Ryder nodded. "It's like you're always on vacation. Not real life."

"Right. He never saw the real me. And once he did, he wasn't so enamored."

Ryder reached over, gripped her thigh, and squeezed. "Because he's an idiot."

She shot him a smile.

"And back to the driving thing," he said. "This isn't my car. If it was, then my ass would be in the driver's seat."

"Do you have a car?"

"I do. I'm a BMW man, myself. I have a sexy i8. And my motorcycle."

She raised her brows. "That sounds expensive."

He shrugged. "I saved all my money when I was in the Air Force. Easton Norcross helped me invest, and I bought a building in Chinatown a few years ago. I did it up slowly, and the rents are good."

"Impressive."

"Yeah, well I still have an impressive mortgage to pay." He leaned closer. "Let me take you out for a fancy dinner once we solve this case. Good food, good wine, you in a spectacular dress."

Her blue gaze met his, direct. It was another thing he liked about her, that she didn't mess around playing games.

"If we close this case, I might let you do that," she said.

He grinned. "I knew I was growing on you."

Once they reached the Norcross Security office, they headed upstairs and straight to Ace's computer room.

The tech guru was leaning back in his chair, eating a bag of potato chips.

"Hi." He flicked the microphone of his head set up. "I wasn't expecting visitors. I'm running searches on similar DBs and got a hit on some results." He nodded to the screens filled with data on the wall. "I sent them to your email, Siv."

"Thanks. We might've found something."

Ryder leaned back on the desk. "A guy who hangs out with Robbie, he was scared, said someone would kill him if he talked."

Ace frowned. "That's not good."

"He said a word," Siv said. "Trelaskin."

Ace dropped his feet to the floor. "Trelaskin?"

"We need to find out who Trelaskin is," Ryder said.

Ace tapped his keyboard, fingers moving fast.

"Nope. No names coming up. Let me try a few different spellings." He leaned forward, groove forming on his brow. "Wait. I've got something."

An article flicked up on the screen. It showed a picture of a couple who looked to be around thirty. The woman wore a fitted, gray, business-style dress, her light-brown hair in a loose bun, with her arms crossed. She was leaning against a man wearing a black turtleneck and black pants. He had a square jaw and serious smile. They both had pale-blue eyes.

The pair was staring earnestly at the camera, looking smart and successful.

"I've seen these two somewhere," Ryder mused.

"Caroline and Christian Foster. Up-and-coming biotech entrepreneurs who are taking Silicon Valley by storm. They're twins, and by all accounts brilliant. They both attended Stanford. From a wealthy family in Washington D.C. Their father is a vice president at a large finance firm, and their mother works at Georgetown University. Caroline and Christian's company, Chiron, has made a breakthrough drug for treating cancer. They say, with the right investment, they can cure all cancer within a decade."

Siv whistled. "Big claim."

Ryder nodded. "Right. I've read the articles about Chiron. Saw the guy give an interview once."

"What's this got to do with Trelaskin?" Siv asked.

"Trelaskin is the name of their wonder drug." Ace tapped a key.

A video flashed up on screen. The twins stood on a large stage with a big screen behind them, dominated by a DNA helix.

"Trelaskin has the power to save our world," Christian Foster intoned.

He was handsome in a bland, everyman way, but with an emphatic look, and a strong, charming voice.

"Imagine if none of us have to lose a loved one to cancer ever again. A mother doesn't die, a father doesn't die, a sibling doesn't die." Caroline's elegant face was filled with emotion.

"No one loses a child," Christian finished. "Never again."

"That's the world—" Caroline spread her arms out "—Chiron, and our drug, Trelaskin, can bring about, with your help."

On the video, the crowd broke into thunderous applause.

Ryder frowned. "What's the status of this 'miracle' drug?"

"Still in preclinical research, it looks like. But the Fosters are busy drumming up investors to take it to the next level. Clinical trials. They want to start testing on humans."

Siv sucked in a breath. "You think Robbie and Scratch were taking Trelaskin?"

Ryder shrugged. "I don't know."

"There's no whiff of rumors that Chiron is up to no good, or using shady practices," Ace said. "Stock prices are up. They have big names on the board. And everyone loves the Fosters."

"Clean-cut, smart, well spoken, and wealthy." Siv shrugged. "The kind of people who inspire trust."

"Why would a tech company be giving their wonder drug to people on the street?" Ryder said.

"Illegal human testing on the vulnerable and disadvantaged has happened before," Ace said. "These companies pay good money." Ace lifted a brow.

Fuck. Ryder got a sick feeling in his gut.

"Trelaskin has one more hurdle before it's approved for human trials." Ace tapped. "They look legit, but I'll dig a little deeper."

"So, they don't seem the type to run illegal human trials," Ryder said.

"Maybe they have a rogue scientist?" Siv suggested.

"Or someone looking to discredit them," Ace added. "From what I can see, the market loves Chiron. The twins are some of the youngest, new billionaires in the country. They have a huge lab out in Palo Alto."

Ryder frowned. "I hope this isn't a fucking dead end."

Robbie deserved justice.

"Hey, it looks like Caroline and Christian Foster are giving a talk this afternoon to potential investors out at the Palo Alto Events Center," Ace said.

Ryder straightened. "We could get a look at them up close and in person." He glanced at Siv. "Can you pull off wealthy investor?"

She crossed her arms. "I can pull off anything, Morgan."

"Okay, then give me your address, go home, and dress up in your best wealthy-woman outfit. I'll pick you up in an hour."

Siv nodded. "You got it."

CHAPTER EIGHT

Stroking her hands down the side of her black skirt, Siv looked at herself in the mirror.

Not bad.

Her white shirt was tucked into her skirt, and the skirt was knee-length and hugged the lines of her body. Her hair was in a twist, with two sticks in it. They looked decorative, but also made really good weapons, if required.

Her makeup was heavier than normal, but professional. She slipped into some low, black heels.

Her gaze fell on a framed photograph on her dresser. It showed two little blonde girls. She was the tall, gangly ten-year-old, while Inger pressed against her side, dainty and petite. Siv's sister was only six in the picture. It was just before she'd gotten sick. Siv pressed a finger to that smiling face.

There was a knock at her front door.

Stepping back, she headed out of her bedroom. She was renting a place in South Beach. The two-bed condo was spacious, with lots of windows that flooded the place with light. The gorgeous, wooden floor had a red tone to it, and she had a great view of the Oracle Park baseball stadium. There was plenty of space for her mom when she came to visit, as she said she was planning to do at Christmas.

Best of all, it was a short walk to the Norcross Security office, and had a pool and a gym, too.

Siv had buzzed Ryder up, so she knew it was him at the door. She swung it open.

Then she almost swallowed her tongue. She thought she'd gotten used to hot guys in suits working at Norcross, but she'd never taken the time to appreciate Ryder Morgan in one.

It was dark blue, and paired with a pale-blue shirt with the collar open. The silver glint of a fancy watch flickered at his wrist. His long hair was pulled back, leaving that handsome face front and center.

Her panties went damp.

God.

His mouth opened, his gaze traveling down her body, then he pretended to clutch his heart. "Ms. Pedersen, you are *gorgeous.*"

She stepped out and closed the door behind her. "I'm sure you say that to all the girls."

"Nope." He reached out and touched the collar of her shirt.

That tantalizing citrus cologne, mixed with his scent, teased her nose.

"If I gave you a sexy set of glasses for you to wear, you'd make all my hot-secretary fantasies come to life."

She snorted. "Really?" They headed for the elevator.

"Yes, I'd be your boss, and I'd definitely be bending you over the desk."

An image of that scenario flashed in her head. She tried to keep her face blank, even though her belly was hot. "I think you should focus on the task ahead."

The elevator opened and they stepped inside.

He let out a breath. "Fine, but I can play the wealthy investor and still fantasize about you. I do that all the time, anyway."

Siv shook her head, wanting to laugh.

Ryder was too charming, too easy to be around. He wasn't scaling her defenses, he was making them melt away.

When they exited her building, the sight of the car parked out front made her stumble to a stop.

The sportscar was sleek, modern-looking, and electric blue.

"That's yours?"

He flashed his sexy smile. "It sure is. BMW i8."

The doors opened up, butterfly style.

"We have to look the part," he said.

She slid inside, and noted him watching her legs as she did.

He circled the car, got in and started the engine. It was silent.

"It's electric?" she asked.

"Hybrid." He pulled out into traffic. "It has a turbocharged 1.5-liter three-cylinder gas engine with an 11.6-kilowatt battery pack and two electric motors. All of that combines for a total of 369 horsepower."

For a man who didn't seem to drive a lot, he was good at it. He zipped through the traffic and obviously knew the car well.

"So, what's our cover story?" she asked.

"We're potential investors. I'm Ryan Moore, and you're Stella Peters. We go in and look rich."

Right. She crossed her legs. "Will we make contact with the Fosters?"

"We'll play it by ear."

They headed south and hit the highway. It took about forty minutes to reach Palo Alto, one of the principal cities of Silicon Valley, and home to numerous headquarters of major tech companies.

When they reached the event center, a steady stream of people in suits were heading into the auditorium. As Ryder parked the car, the i8 gained quite a few covetous glances.

Siv slid out and straightened her skirt.

"Let's go, Stella." He took her arm and tucked it into his.

"I don't think business associates hold arms."

He just smiled at her.

They headed inside. The large banners in the lobby featured images of the Fosters. Christian was in his trademark black turtleneck, channeling Steve Jobs. Caroline looked svelte and elegant in a fitted, gray pantsuit.

The auditorium was large, and quickly filling up. She and Ryder took their seats, just as the lights dimmed.

"Welcome," a warm female voice said. "I hope you're ready to help make tomorrow's future a reality today." Caroline walked out in a navy-blue dress and matching heels. Images flashed on the massive screen behind her. They showed a history of medicine in old black-and-white pictures. Old hospital wards, Marie Curie in her lab, nurses in old-fashioned uniforms. The images flashed faster and faster, showing medicine and equipment getting more modern and advanced. Soon, there were full-color images of modern hospitals and research labs. The slideshow finally stopped on a smiling child, with a small, medical patch on her arm with the Chiron logo on it—a stylized, circular twist of lines.

"That's right," a deep male voice said. "With *your* help, we can end the fight against cancer." Christian stalked in from the other side of the stage.

"That guy must own a lot of turtlenecks," Ryder murmured.

Siv's lips twitched.

The Fosters launched into their opening spiel. Pictures of them as kids flashed up, then at school and at Stanford. They were charming, eloquent, and made you want to trust them.

Siv didn't like them at all.

They reminded her too much of her father and Johan. All flash, with no substance underneath.

They started to talk about their research. Pictures of labs packed full of lab-coat wearing scientists appeared.

"Our dedicated team is working around the clock to get Trelaskin ready for human trials," Caroline said. "We are on the cusp of changing the lives of *so* many."

"I'm not sure I'm buying this story," Siv whispered. "They're too slick."

Ryder grunted.

"But what they're hoping to achieve..." An old, faded sadness welled inside her.

"Hey." Ryder took her hand. "You lost someone to cancer?"

"Most people have brushed up against it." She knew she should pull away, but she left her hand in his. "I had a younger sister. Inger. She died of leukemia when she was seven." It had been the death knell for her parents' shaky marriage, although knowing her father, he would've already been sleeping with his assistant.

Ryder squeezed her fingers.

"I would've given anything for something like Trelaskin," she said.

"Yeah, if it is as good as they say..."

The Fosters finished to loud applause. Christian took his sister's hand and they gave a small bow.

Ryder rose and tugged Siv up.

"So, Ms. Peters, shall we have a chat with our hosts?"

Siv smoothed her skirt. "Yes, Mr. Moore. An excellent idea."

A LOT of people liked the Foster twins. There was a small crowd of people around them, all vying for the chance to talk with the pair.

As Ryder and Siv approached, he saw them smiling and nodding. Caroline pressed a hand to a woman's arm, sympathy on her face.

"I'm so sorry that you lost your daughter. Stories like

yours drive me. Inspire me to work toward a world without cancer."

Caroline's gaze flicked up and hit Ryder. He saw the spark of appreciation and he made himself smile back.

He grabbed Siv's hand and pulled her closer. Finally, they reached the pair.

"A fabulous presentation," Ryder smiled. "It's wonderful work you're doing."

"Thank you." Christian's smile was wide and well-practiced. It reminded Ryder of a politician.

When he did a poor job of eyeing Siv's legs, Ryder felt less friendly.

"I'm Ryan Moore. A local businessman. We're always looking for good investments." He smiled. "Not only with a good return, but one that can change people's lives, like your drug."

"Excellent. We need all the help we can to bring Trelaskin safely to market." Christian eyed Siv. "And who's your colleague?"

Siv shot the man a smile. "I'm Stella—"

"Stella Peters." Ryder slid an arm around her. "My wife, business partner, and love of my life." He kissed her temple.

He didn't miss the flicker of annoyance in her eyes, but she was good and hid it fast.

She'd make him pay later.

He couldn't wait.

"Lovely." Christian poorly hid his disappointment. "Caro, darling, meet Mr. Ryan Moore and his wife Stella."

"It's Ryan," Ryder said.

"A pleasure," Caroline drawled. She held Ryder's hand a little too long.

"We enjoyed your presentation," Siv said. "Truly a cause we can get behind."

Caroline smiled serenely. "We're happy to hear that."

"I'd like to take a closer look at your trial results," Siv said.

"Stella's the brains of our operation." Ryder squeezed her closer. "She has degrees in science and biotechnology."

The twins' smiles stayed pinned in place.

Christian inclined his head. "Brains and beauty. Of course. Everything is in our prospectus. Trelaskin has a little way to go, but the results are so incredibly promising."

Caroline cocked her head. "What business are you in, Ryan?"

He smiled. "Tech, some property. I like to dabble."

Siv's laugh was a tinkle. "He likes to make money."

"Busted. But I love you more." He pressed a quick kiss to her lips.

He felt the twins watching them.

"It's wonderful to see such a committed relationship," Christian said. "It's rare these days."

"I wouldn't be where I am without my Ryan." Out of view of the Fosters, Siv pinched his side. Then she turned back to the pair. "So, your research is done at your Palo Alto lab. Is it possible to get a tour?"

"Our facilities are state of the art," Christian said.

"We're so proud of our lab," Caroline gushed. "But

I'm afraid we don't do tours. To protect our work. Corporate espionage is a real problem."

Christian nodded, face solemn. "We're investing so much money, time, resources—"

"—and heart," Caroline added.

Her brother touched her arm. "Of course. And it's not just us. All our investors who are helping us realize a healthier future have a lot at stake."

"So, no tours," Caroline said. "We invest in some of the best security to keep the lab and our work safe and secure."

"Well, that's a shame, but understandable," Siv murmured. "I look forward to going over your prospectus."

Both twins flashed smiles.

Caroline touched Ryder's arm, fingers stroking. "And we hope to have you on board as partners on this incredible, and vitally important, journey."

Siv leaned into Ryder, and pressed a hand to his chest. "Ryan and I will go over everything on Chiron and Trelaskin in great detail. Won't we, darling?"

He was a little distracted by the feel of her hand on his chest. He cupped her jaw and saw the flare of something molten in her eyes. His fingers brushed her neck, and he felt her pulse racing. "Yes, we will."

But his gut clenched. The little faker. She'd been banging on about not being interested in him, but her pulse said something else. She wasn't quite so cool under that sleek, Norwegian exterior.

"Of course," Caroline said. "We look forward to hearing from you soon."

Ryder took Siv's hand, and other people pushed forward to talk to the twins. Siv and Ryder headed out into the sunny day.

"What did you think?" he asked, as they walked toward the car.

"I don't like them, although I can't say exactly why. They're just too slick, too practiced, and too polished."

"Yeah, they're really pushing the successful, young entrepreneur thing hard."

"I guess that's what gets people to hand over their money." Siv cocked her head. "Caroline sure liked the look of you."

They reached the car and he smiled at her over the roof. "Legions of women do, my Norwegian flower."

Siv rolled her eyes, then she scanned the car. "Can I drive?"

The doors opened. "Not on your life."

They strapped in and he started the car. Ryder headed back toward the city and the Norcross office.

"If their drug can do what they say, then it will be amazing," Siv said quietly.

The look on her face said that she was thinking of her sister. "Yeah. A part of me hopes this has nothing to do with Robbie's death."

"The info they give out will look good, won't it?"

Ryder nodded. "Right. They'll only show all the good stuff to potential investors. Ace can probably dig deeper and check that it's legit."

He touched the dash and the call went through.

"Hey, Ryder." Ace's voice echoed through the car. "How did it go?"

"The Fosters are as shiny as their dental veneers. It all sounded good. You turn up anything?"

"I'm poking around their system. I can't crack their lab in Palo Alto though. It has a hell of a cyber security system on it, including non-networked machines."

"It makes sense." Ryder tapped his fingers on the wheel. "They're keeping their research heavily protected."

"Wall Street loves them. The business magazines and conferences are full of them. There are murmurs they'll be on the cover of Time."

Siv crossed her arms. "I don't like them."

"They're looking legit. Wait." Ace paused. "Shit, I just intercepted an email. Christian Foster has asked his security team to look into you two, or your aliases, and a few other potential investors."

"Fuck," Ryder said.

"Ace, are you on this?" Siv asked.

"Hell, yeah. I'll have to work fast and plant an online back story for you both."

"We're married and in love, by the way," Ryder said.

"Congratulations," Ace said, sounding amused.

"Stella kept her maiden name, and she's also got degrees in science and biotechnology."

"I'll make sure to put that in."

"Keep us posted." Ryder ended the call and then drummed his fingers on the steering wheel. "There is only one way we'll find out what we need on Trelaskin."

"How?" she asked.

"We get into Chiron's lab and take a little look around."

A smile curved her lips. "Are you suggesting a little B and E, Morgan?"

"Why, yes I am, Pedersen."

She paused. "I should go in with one of the other Norcross guys. This is more my thing than yours."

Hell, no. He wasn't going to be left behind. "But I'm the one with the medical knowledge. I'll know what to look for. Besides, while I don't work in private security, I'm not inexperienced, Siv."

She took a breath, then finally nodded. "You have to follow my lead."

He grinned. "I'll happily follow you anywhere."

CHAPTER NINE

Night had fallen when Siv parked the X6 two blocks from the Chiron lab in Palo Alto.

Ryder was meeting her here. She stepped out and pulled a small, black backpack onto her shoulder. She was in black jeans and a black, long-sleeved T-shirt.

And ready to take a look inside Chiron's lab.

"Hey."

She barely controlled her reaction. She hadn't heard Ryder at all.

She turned, and in the glow from a nearby streetlight, she saw Ryder, wearing dark-green cargo pants, and a black shirt.

"Hi," she said.

"You got that doohickey that Ace gave you?"

"The *doohickey* is some fancy piece of tech that's going to get him into Chiron's system." Ace had entrusted her with the tiny, metallic circle that was smaller than a button battery. And he'd given her detailed instructions on attaching it to a computer.

"Shall we?" Ryder waved an arm.

They headed down the dark street, sticking to the shadows. They were in an industrial area of Palo Alto, where a lot of companies had research centers and laboratories. It was still pretty nice, with wide, tree-lined streets, and sprawling, two-story buildings with lots of glass.

Soon, the lab appeared ahead. A fancy sign at the front had Chiron engraved on it.

They paused in the shadows under a tree.

"You went over the schematics?" she murmured.

Ryder nodded.

"I suggest we climb the fence on that side." She pointed. "There's a gap in the camera coverage. Ace is going to work his magic on the internal cameras once we get him in the system. So, we have to sneak in, find a computer, and plant Ace's bug as quickly as we can."

"How are we getting in the door?"

She held up a key card. "Ace sorted it out."

"Guards?"

She nodded. "Four. Two patrolling outside, two inside."

Ryder pulled in a breath and grinned. "Let's do this."

They hurried toward the fence.

Behind the steel fence was a modern, glass building nestled among some simple landscaping. It looked like any other building in the area.

Siv grabbed his arm and pointed. A shadowed figure turned a corner of the building and disappeared into the night.

"Go," she murmured.

They reached the fence, right where there was a

narrow gap in the cameras. She gripped the metal and climbed quickly. She dropped down on the other side in the parking area in a crouch.

A second later, Ryder landed beside her.

His smile was white in the darkness. He looked like he was enjoying himself.

Her blood was singing, as well. It felt like forever since she'd been on a mission. "Follow me exactly until we reach the building."

He nodded.

She eyed the camera locations, then jogged toward the building. When she reached it, she pressed her back toward the glass. Ryder landed beside her.

"Won't the cameras catch us at the front door?" he asked.

"Yes, but once we're in, Ace will wipe the footage. We have to move fast. We've got three minutes before the guards will be back to monitor the camera feed and spot us. We get in, plant the bug, and let Ace do his thing."

Ryder ran a hand down her arm. "I'll be right behind you."

And she realized that she trusted that he would be there, having her back.

Siv shoved that thought down to ponder later. She moved to the front doors, then swiped the card through the reader. The lock beeped and the glass doors slid open.

"Let's move," she murmured.

They hurried through the reception area. It was sleek, with lots of gray and wood. A huge Chiron logo dominated one wall.

They paused at the internal doors. There was no

sound beyond the glossy reception area. Siv nudged the door open. The hall beyond was all white-tiled floors and muted-blue walls.

"We need to look for an office with a computer," she said.

They moved down the hall, quickly opening doors. Coffee room. Conference room.

"Here," Ryder said.

It was a small, very sterile-looking, office. The walls were a plain white, and there were no framed photos, or collectibles. Siv sat on the desk chair and then woke the monitor. The Chiron logo glowed. *Perfect.*

She slid the small bug from her pocket and stuck it under the monitor, where it wouldn't be noticed.

She touched her earpiece. "Ace, the bug is in place."

"Okay," the tech guru said. "Give me a second. I'm accessing the device so I can piggyback on the Chiron system."

She and Ryder waited.

"Utilizing a backdoor and...I'm in. Give me a second to locate the security system."

Siv resisted the urge to tap her foot. She'd spent so many moments like this one, in the field, in danger of being discovered, waiting for her chance to attack. She glanced up at Ryder. He didn't look fazed either.

"The cameras are disabled," Ace said.

Siv rose. "Let's take a look at the lab." She opened the office door.

"Crap, there's a guard heading your way," Ace said.

Shit. She and Ryder froze. She closed the office door slowly.

A moment later, they heard footsteps and someone whistling, then they were gone.

"Clear," Ace said.

With a nod, Siv cautiously stepped into the hallway. They moved quickly, away from the guard, and deeper into the building.

"There," Ryder said.

A sign on the doors said *Laboratories*.

They slipped through the doors. In the next corridor were long, glass windows on either side, and neat, pristine labs behind the glass.

Too pristine.

She frowned. "The workbenches are all empty." It looked nothing like the photos Caroline and Christian had shown at the investor event. There was no equipment, no test work, nothing.

"Maybe they aren't using these labs, or they pack everything up at night?" Ryder suggested, not sounding convinced.

"Are there more labs upstairs?" Siv asked Ace.

"The labs are on this level," Ace said. "Upstairs is all offices."

Siv and Ryder moved along the corridor. The next set of labs were just as clean and empty.

It didn't look like a hive of research activity to Siv.

Ryder's frown deepened. "Let's take a closer look."

He pushed the door to the closest lab open.

There were low lights on inside. The workbenches were completely devoid of equipment and materials. Siv touched the stainless-steel surface. It was covered in a thin layer of dust.

"No one's used this room in a while," Siv said.

Ryder headed for a computer at the end of one workbench and touched his ear. "Ace, we need to access the computer in lab C3."

"Hang on," Ace said. "There you go."

The screen blinked on, the Chiron logo displayed in the center. Ryder leaned over and tapped the keyboard.

Siv kept an eye on the corridor. The guards weren't due to do rounds for another twenty minutes, but it paid to be careful.

Ryder hissed.

"What?" Siv didn't see any information on the screen.

"There's nothing here."

She frowned. "What you mean?"

"No tests. No data. No lab supplies. Limited equipment." He met her gaze. "There are no scientists doing work in this lab."

Siv blinked. "What the hell?"

"I can confirm," Ace said in their ears. "There's no testing going on. I checked entry logs for the building. Only the security guards and the odd visitor are in and out of the building each day. There's no other staff."

Siv shoved her hands on her hips. "The Fosters are a fraud."

"Sure looks that way," Ace said.

"Assholes!" Siv said. "They're preying on people's desperate hopes to save their loved ones."

"And they might be worse monsters, if we can link their drug to Robbie's death," Ryder said darkly.

"If they are running illegal tests, they must have data somewhere," Siv said.

"The Fosters own a bunch of properties around San Francisco," Ace said. "But no labs that I can see."

"They'd need a lab to make batches of the drug," Ryder said.

"I don't understand." Siv shook her head. "Why have this lab here? And lie about it?"

"Money. Greed. Appearances." A muscle in Ryder's jaw ticked. "Whatever happens, they are going down."

"Fuck, guys, a guard is coming," Ace bit out. "He's almost at your location!"

Hell. Ryder reached for the computer, but Siv spotted movement in the hall.

"No time." She yanked Ryder down behind the workbench, and they crawled along the floor.

A door opened. "Why is there a computer on in here?" a man's voice said from the doorway.

Footsteps entered the lab.

Faen. Ryder reached past her. There was a shelf under the workbench. He squeezed his big frame in, and urged her to follow.

She climbed on and pressed against him. They were wedged together in the small space.

He slid an arm around her.

Then, the guard walked right past them.

FUCKING HELL. Ryder held on to Siv, trying to keep his breathing even.

She felt relaxed, but alert. They listened to the guard mutter and turn the monitor off. The man paused, as if he was scanning the empty lab.

"Must've turned itself on," the man muttered.

"Joe?" The squawk of a radio. "Any problems?"

"Negative, Rich," the guard answered. "All quiet, as usual."

With a grunt, Joe the guard stomped out.

Ryder released a breath, adrenaline pumping through his veins.

"That was close," Siv said.

Screw it. He cupped her jaw, tipped her head back and kissed her.

Ryder figured he'd get an elbow to the gut, but she shocked him. She slid her hands into his hair and kissed him back.

It was hot, heavy, and way too short.

She pulled back and licked her lips. "Let's get out of here."

Ryder nodded. There was no data for them to collect. Frustration burned hotly in his gut.

Something was definitely off at Chiron, but fraud was a long way from murder.

They crept out of the lab and back into the corridor. Unsurprisingly, Siv moved with obvious ease and experience. Her special-forces work showed.

He dragged his gaze off her legs. At the end of the corridor, she held up a fist and he paused. She checked the next corridor, then waved him forward.

They moved silently toward a side exit. The sound of whistling caught his ear, and they froze. It wasn't too close, but it was echoing off the tiles somewhere not too far away, either.

Siv picked up speed and turned down another corridor. She touched her ear. "Ace, confirming secondary exit is clear, and the alarm is disabled."

"You're good to go," Ace murmured.

Siv opened the door, and she and Ryder slipped into the night.

They paused with their backs to the wall of the building.

"Wait." She watched the far corner of the building, then glanced at her watch. "There should be a guard."

Somewhere in the distance, Ryder heard the drone of traffic, and the wail of a siren. It was an ambulance—he knew the sound all too well.

He forced himself not to fidget. His blood was humming, running hot.

"The guard should be exiting this area," Siv said.

He heard the frown in her voice. There was no sign of any guard.

"Maybe he went to take a leak?" Ryder said.

"I don't like it. If we move, we risk running into him."

They waited another minute. No guard appeared.

She straightened. "Okay, no choice left. Let's make a move. Straight for the fence."

She took off at a run. Ryder followed. Damn, those long legs of hers...

They reached the fence. Siv pressed a hand to the metal, just as a shout cut through the night.

"Hey, this is private property!" A beam of a flashlight cut their way.

Fuck. The out-of-sync guard had spotted them.

The man ran at them. "Stay where you are!"

Siv swiveled, then attacked. Her kicks sent the guard staggering into the fence. The air rushed out of him with an *oof*.

Ryder stepped in. His punch landed in the man's soft gut, making him drop the flashlight.

Siv kicked the guard again, but he partially blocked it and recovered enough to half turn and grab her leg.

Shit. Ryder stiffened.

But he didn't need to worry. He watched Siv break into a combination of kicks and hits. She moved like damn liquid—grace and lethal beauty.

The guard collapsed with a groan.

"Go," Siv said. "*Go.*"

They both hit the fence and climbed.

"Ace, a guard intercepted us at the fence," Siv said.

"Acknowledged. I'll mess with the camera footage. They'll believe you climbed the fence, but got no farther."

"Thanks. Signing off now."

Ryder slipped his earpiece out as they jogged down the sidewalk.

"Where's your car?" she asked.

"Around the corner from yours."

They slowed to a walk, moving quietly through the night.

"The Fosters are phonies," she said.

"It looks that way."

"But we haven't linked them to Robbie. It doesn't even look like they're making drugs."

"Ace is in the system now. If the link is there, he'll find it." Ryder would have to hold on to that.

His car appeared out of the darkness.

Siv stopped. "You drove your fancy, very noticeable i8 to a B and E?"

He grinned. God, he loved that tone. "Babe, there are loads of hot cars around here. Besides, no one will expect the driver of this beauty to be breaking into anything."

She touched the hood. "It is a hell of a car."

"It was hot watching you take down that guard." Desire was like a blowtorch to his system.

She eyed him with an intensity that he felt deeply.

"You really mean that, don't you?" she asked.

Confused, he frowned. "Why wouldn't I?"

"Damn, you make it hard."

"What hard?" He had no idea what she was talking about.

She advanced on him until her body pressed against his. His ass hit the hood of his car and she stepped between his legs.

"Siv—"

"Quiet." She cupped his face and kissed him.

Hell. He yanked her closer, tongue diving into her mouth. He slid one hand to cradle the back of her head, the other to cup her ass.

The excitement and adrenaline of the night, mixed with his constant desire for her, exploded.

She kissed him back with a hell of a lot of energy and enthusiasm. Her moan made his gut clench. Her tongue stroked his.

More. He needed more.

He forced her delectable mouth wider and deepened the kiss. She rubbed against him, and his cock was as hard as steel behind his zipper.

She made a hungry sound.

Desperate, he spun them, pressing her back against the hood of his car.

"God, you get me hot," she panted.

"You've done a good job of telling me otherwise." He yanked her legs around his hips and his cock pressed against the seam of her jeans.

She reared up, jerking in his hold, breathing fast.

"Damn, you're close, aren't you?" he gritted out.

"Yes. You seem to do that to me."

"I'm going to make you come, Siv." He unfastened her jeans. "You're going to say my name when you splinter apart."

She bit her lip. Ryder slid his hand inside her jeans and panties.

"*Ah.*" She bucked and bit her lip harder.

Damn. He stroked her.

"You're so wet, Siv. You want me so badly, don't you? You want my cock inside you." He slid two fingers into her tight warmth.

"Oh, God." Her hips moved.

"That's it." His thumb found her swollen clit.

He didn't care that they were outside. The world disappeared. Cloaked by darkness, here in this back street in an industrial area, there was no one to see them.

He kept working her.

"Siv, you're going to feel like heaven when I finally

work my cock inside you. It'll stretch you, you'll bite your lip, like you're doing now."

"Don't stop," she sobbed.

"Not until you come." He leaned over and kissed her.

Her body tensed, then she came. "Ryder!"

Her voice was sweet music to his ears. He watched the pleasure wash over her. God, he nearly came in his pants.

He watched her slump on his car, her eyelashes fluttering.

Then he saw something he hadn't expected. A flash of uncertainty in her eyes.

A part of him was happy he was getting to her. He pulled his hand free and re-did her jeans. As he watched, she tried to compose herself.

She cleared her throat. "My place or yours, Morgan?"

Ah. She was rebuilding her shields. He should've expected that. He reminded himself that nothing worth having ever came easy.

He stroked her cheek. "Not tonight."

She blinked, frowned. "What?"

"You want hot sex, then you'll kick me out of your bed and brush it off."

"No—"

He pulled her off the car and kissed her nose, enjoying the confusion in her eyes. "I want more than sex. More than one night, Siv."

Now he saw something he really hadn't expected. A flash of fear.

Then he did the hardest thing he'd ever done in his life. "Get in the car. I'll drop you back at the X6."

CHAPTER TEN

The next morning, Ryder sipped his coffee, whistling to himself.

It was sunny, but the air felt cooler. The fall was making itself felt.

He strode down the street, nodding to Mrs. Kwan in the doorway of her restaurant. She gave him a wave.

His mind was full of Siv Pedersen.

Hot, tough, sexy Siv.

He'd drifted off to sleep the night before, thinking about her. The way she sounded when she came, the way she'd clenched on his fingers.

Hell. He needed to get a lock on this vicious need. He had shit to do, starting with asking a few more questions around the neighborhood.

If he could, he'd find Scratch again. Ask about the drug and the Fosters. Check that he was okay.

Ryder planned to visit a few places around the Tenderloin, then he'd drop by the Norcross Security office with some blueberry buns. He fished his phone out of his jeans and tapped out a message.

I hope you slept well.

Siv didn't make him wait long.

I did.

Ah, his woman of few words.

Any word from Ace?

He's combing through what little data was at the lab, and going through the Foster's properties. No secret lab...yet. He's on his second coffee and cursing a lot.

If there's anything to find, he'll find it. So, what are you wearing?

Are you really that clichéd?

When it comes to you, yes.

His phone dinged. It was a picture of a pant-clad leg and a high-heel boot.

Ooh, a sexy pantsuit. He added a heart-eyes emoji.

Morgan, it doesn't take much with you.

My Norwegian flower, with you, it requires you to just be breathing.

He could almost see her eye roll from where he stood.

Where are you?

Heading out to find Scratch and ask a few more questions. Want to join me?

Can't. I need to help Ace, or he might stop my phone from working or something. Be careful.

Aww, you're worried about me. I'll see you later.

He slid the phone away and finished his coffee.

Right. Time to find some answers.

Ace and Siv were working to find out if the Fosters had a working lab somewhere else. Ryder would find out once and for all if Robbie had been taking Trelaskin.

Ryder stopped by a few haunts. He checked in with a few familiar faces he knew. No one had seen Scratch.

He ended up at the Hot Zone. He spotted a woman who came into the clinic sporadically. Annie had a big mix of mental health issues.

"Hi, Annie."

She wouldn't make eye contact with him, and her hands fluttered. "Oh. Ryder from the clinic. Hi, Ryder."

He sat down, but left a large gap so he didn't make her nervous. "That's right." He kept his tone gentle, non-threatening. "How have you been?"

"Good. Good. I found lots of food lately."

"Glad to hear it." As always, he felt sorry for her. He wished things were different. As far as he knew, her family had disowned her. "If you need anything, you can drop by the clinic."

She dipped her head shyly. "Thanks."

"Hey, have you seen Scratch?"

Her shy smile vanished and her fingers twisted. She

was clearly upset. "Nope. No. No Scratch." She looked at the ground.

"I'm your friend, Annie. And I'm Scratch's friend. I'm trying to help him."

She lowered her voice. "He was real scared. He felt sick."

Shit. Ryder should've walked Scratch to the clinic himself.

"People are looking for him," Annie whispered. "He was scared."

"Who's after him?"

"I don't know." She twisted her fingers, rocking a little. "I don't know."

"Okay, Annie." Crap, Ryder hoped someone hadn't hurt Scratch. "What about Robbie, Annie?"

"Robbie's gone. I don't want him to be gone. He gave me candy. He stopped people hurting me."

Robbie had left a hole in so many lives. "I know. I miss him, too. You know what he was doing before he died?"

Her rocking increased.

Crap. Ryder straightened. Did she know something? "Annie. You could help me find the people who hurt Robbie."

She made a sound. "I saw him with some people."

"Okay."

"Fancy men."

"Fancy? You mean they were clean and wearing nice clothes?"

She nodded. "Suits."

"His brother—"

"No, no. Different. Big. Bigger than you." She held her arms up like a bodybuilder.

"Muscular guys." Someone's muscle. "Was anyone else with them?"

She bit her nails. They were dirty and bleeding.

"Annie? Was there another man with them?"

"No. A woman. She got out of the fancy car. She looked mad at Robbie."

Ryder's pulse spiked. "A woman."

"In a dress. Fancy. Brown hair pulled up fancy."

"Hang on—" He pulled his phone out.

"I have to go." Annie rose, fidgeting.

"Annie, was this the fancy woman?" He held up a picture of the Fosters with some other tech entrepreneurs.

Annie's nose wrinkled. "Fancy." She nodded and tapped on Caroline. "That's the fancy lady."

Elation shot through him. *A link.* A link to Caroline Foster, who'd been talking to Robbie.

"I have to go." Annie hurriedly gathered her shopping bags filled with various things and dumped them into a shopping cart. "Scratch was scared of the fancy people. Be careful, Ryder from the clinic."

"Thanks, Annie. And if you see Scratch, tell him to come to the clinic."

Annie hurried off, pushing the cart.

Ryder left the encampment and texted Siv.

Woman on the street saw Robbie talking with two guys in suits and Caroline Foster.

His phone vibrated.

You're sure?

Annie picked Caroline out of the photo.

Good! We're right on track, Morgan.

I'm on my way to Norcross. I want to see that pantsuit.

You'd like what I'm wearing under it even more.

He grinned. She was flirting with him.

Now I'm hard.

You're so easy.

See you soon. I expect a hello kiss.

We'll see.

That's not a no.

Ryder turned the corner, and spotted two thugs waiting for him. It was Tattoo Guy and Shaggy Hair.

Ryder straightened. "You back for more?"

"You're all alone, asshole. And asking questions our employer doesn't want asked."

"I don't give a fuck," Ryder bit out. "And I can handle you two with my eyes closed."

Tattoo Guy grinned. "Ah, but we aren't alone." He looked past Ryder.

Ryder glanced back over his shoulder. Three big guys moved in. They looked mean and ready for a fight.

Oh, fuck.

He braced. Across the street, some people saw the impending fight brewing and scuffled away. No one would help in the Tenderloin.

One man lunged. Ryder swiveled and grabbed the guy. He swung the guy around and slammed him into a second guy.

The third man charged, and Ryder kicked him in the gut.

A punch landed in Ryder's lower back and pain rocketed through him. He gritted his teeth.

His focus narrowed to the fight. It was all fierce punches, kicks, and groans.

A punch hit his jaw and he tasted blood.

Tattoo Guy and Shaggy Hair rushed him together, and he tried to block, but several punches landed. One hit his stomach.

Pain exploded and he realized that the asshole was wearing brass knuckles.

Fucking hell.

Ryder fought back, but the next blow knocked him to his knees. Kicks followed, pain drowning him.

He heard shouts, but a kick hit his head and he slumped to the concrete.

His body was just a throb of horrible pain.

More shouts.

He saw boots running away, but everything was dimming.

Then his vision turned black.

WHERE THE HELL WAS RYDER? He should've reached the office by now.

Siv watched Ace working at his computer. She blew out a breath. Memories of what she and Ryder had done on the hood of his fancy car kept playing through her head. Her own X-rated movie. She'd come so hard.

She'd come hard again in her own bed, touching herself and wishing Ryder had been there.

She heard Ace bite out some words in Portuguese, which had to be curses. She shook her head to clear it and stalked over to his chair.

"What's wrong?"

"Someone's digging hard on yours and Ryder's aliases." The tech man swiveled. "They're picking Ryan Moore and Stella Peters apart."

She cursed.

"I'm keeping one step ahead of them for now." Ace lifted his tablet and tapped. "Time to give the big man an update."

A few minutes later, Vander appeared in the doorway.

"Sit rep?" His rugged face was blank, focused.

"Either Ryder and I set off alarm bells, or the Fosters really dig deep on the potential investors," she said.

"Most of the focus has been on Moore and Peter's 'businesses.'"

"They're most interested in the money," Vander said.

Ace nodded. "Looks like it." He tapped the keyboard. "I did find this."

It was a picture of a guy standing on a sidewalk, smoking a cigarette.

"One of the Fosters' security team. He's an ex-Army Ranger and he's standing outside the fake address of Moore and Peters."

Vander cursed.

Siv's muscles tightened. "He's waiting for us to come home. Ryder and I need to make an appearance as the happy couple."

"Yes. If they can check off the boxes, hopefully they'll quit digging," Ace said. "I'll spread the word that you guys have been in Napa, looking to buy a vineyard."

"Oh yes, I like buying vineyards," Siv said. "The wine tastes so much better when you own it."

The men laughed.

"Who owns the property you used as their home address?" Vander asked.

"It's one of your investment apartments," Ace said. "In Nob Hill."

Vander swiveled. "Siv, you and Ryder need to stay there for a couple of nights. Sell Moore and Peters as a couple."

Great. She dragged in a breath. "Sure." She frowned. "Ryder was supposed to be here by now. I'll give him a call." She pulled out her cell phone and found his number.

The phone rang and rang. *What the hell was he doing?*

Then the call connected.

"Hey, where are you?" she asked.

There was no reply.

She frowned. "Ryder?"

Then she heard raspy, pained breathing.

Her pulse spiked. "Ryder, what's wrong? Talk to me? Are you all right?"

She sensed Vander and Ace's attention sharpen.

"Ryder?"

The line went dead.

"*Faen*!" she cursed, her pulse going haywire.

"Siv?" Vander barked.

"Ace, track Ryder's phone." She swallowed, her mouth dry and her chest tight. "He didn't talk, but he sounded in pain."

"Fuck," Vander said.

Ace's fingers were flying. "Give me a sec. He has a Norcross cell phone with a tracker in it." A map flashed up on the screen. "*There*."

She eyed it. The glowing dot was in the Tenderloin.

Vander's jaw tightened. "An alley. I'm coming with you."

Unsurprisingly, Vander claimed the driver's seat of the X6.

Siv's hands clenched into fists as Vander sped toward the Tenderloin. *Be okay, Morgan. Please be okay*.

If he was badly hurt, or worse...

No. Siv couldn't imagine a world without Ryder Morgan's sexy smile and charm in it.

He'd be fine. He had to be.

Vander broke the speed limits where he could, and finally screeched to a halt on a dirty street in the Tenderloin.

Before the SUV was fully stopped, Siv flung the door open. She saw a crowd of homeless people in the alley.

No. She sprinted over.

"Hey, that's Ryder's woman," someone muttered.

She thought she recognized a few faces.

When the tense crowd backed up, looking wary, she knew Vander was behind her.

That's when she saw Ryder sprawled on the ground.

Her heart hit her ribs.

A man with an unkempt beard was crouched beside him. *Bish.*

She raced over. "Ryder."

He was lying facedown. Vander crouched beside her, and they rolled him onto his side.

"Some guys jumped him." Bish's voice trembled. "Big guys. Five of them. Had metal knuckles on their hands."

God. If they'd beaten him, he could have internal injuries. She saw several dirty footprints on Ryder's shirt and rage welled.

They'd *kicked* him.

She checked his pulse and found it beating strongly. *Thank God.* She cupped his jaw. There was blood at the corner of his mouth and swelling around one eye.

"Ryder?"

His eyes opened, swimming in pain. "There's my Norwegian angel."

Vander snorted. "He sounds okay."

Siv ripped his shirt open and sucked in a breath. Bruises were forming all over his torso.

"What happened?" she asked.

A couple of homeless people pushed forward. "Some

gangbangers cornered him," a black woman said. "He hurt a few of them real good. They had to carry two of 'em out of here."

Siv probed and Ryder grunted.

"But there were five of them," Bish continued. "We rushed in, yelling, to scare 'em off Ryder."

"Thanks, Bish," Ryder croaked. "Thanks, all of you."

"You're too pretty to let someone mess up that face," a woman called out.

Ryder grinned, but when it pulled his lip, he grimaced. "Help me up?"

Vander and Siv got him sitting upright. She saw he was trying to hide his pain.

And she was having trouble hiding just how churned up she was that he'd been hurt.

"Was it those guys from before?" she asked.

"Yeah, but they brought some friends."

"I'll bring the SUV around." Vander jogged off.

Siv touched Ryder's shoulder, because she needed the contact. "We'll get you to the hospital—"

"No. I don't need the hospital."

"Morgan, don't be a macho idiot. You could have internal bleeding—"

He cupped her cheek. "Worried about me, Siv?"

She was. "No matter how annoying you are, I don't want you dying."

"Not going to die. And I'm not being macho. I'm a combat medic and I can assess my injuries. I'm bruised to hell, but I'm not bleeding internally. I just need some painkillers and an ice pack or three."

She pressed her lips together.

He rubbed a thumb over her skin. "I promise."

"Well, you're going to have to rest and recuperate at Stella Moore and Ryan Peters' love nest."

His brows drew together. "Huh?"

"The Fosters are poking around our aliases. We need to make an appearance at 'our' place."

"Shit. They have someone watching?"

She nodded.

The X6 pulled up at the mouth of the alley.

She helped Ryder to his feet, taking some of his weight.

"Looks like you're going to be stuck with me as your nurse," she said.

"The day's looking up."

CHAPTER ELEVEN

Okay, it was official, he felt like shit.

Ryder sat back on the couch, wincing. He wasn't surprised to find Vander's Nob Hill apartment was nice.

It was on the seventeenth floor, and a corner apartment, so there were windows everywhere. Bright-white walls contrasted with the wide-plank wood floors. The windows had black frames, which made all the kick-ass views of the city look like artwork. The furnishings were sleek and modern, but still comfortable. The open-plan living, dining, and kitchen area was long and spacious and tall, green indoor plants here and there added some color.

Vander had dropped them off. First, he'd stopped by their apartments, and Siv had collected some clothes and toiletries for them. Vander had also left the first aid kit from the X6. For now, this was home for the loved-up Ryan and Stella.

Siv was out making sure she was seen by the Fosters'

security guy. Ryder struggled with his shirt and finally got it off. He was a mass of throbbing pain.

He heard the front door open, and a second later, Siv strode in holding a shopping bag. Her gaze went straight to him, running over his bare chest before settling on his bruises. Her face darkened and she swiveled, and headed for the kitchen.

"This place is gorgeous," she said, opening the fridge.

Ryder grunted. "Yeah, Vander owns a few investment properties. Easton has more. I think he owns half the damn city." He watched her fill a glass with water. "Did you spot the Foster's guy?"

"Yeah. He wasn't trying very hard to be stealthy. Stella walked past him twice, and stopped close by to take a phone call."

"My wife is so badass."

Her head jerked up, and she eyed him for a beat. Then she came back with a glass of water in one hand and two ice packs in the other.

"Take these." She handed him the glass and tipped two pills onto his palm.

Ryder did as ordered.

She sat beside him, wrapped the first ice pack in a towel, and pressed it to his side.

He hissed.

"Hold that." She wrapped the second one and pressed it to his collarbone where a lovely lump and bruise had formed.

Ryder eyed her bent head.

"You'd make a great nurse. You don't have one of those little white dresses and hats, do you?"

She shot him a look sharp enough to slice.

He laughed, absorbing the pain it caused. "I didn't think so, but it was worth a try."

Siv rolled her eyes. "How's the pain?"

"Manageable."

She reached out and touched another bruise lightly. "I don't like seeing you beat up, Morgan."

"I'm not a fan myself."

Then she shocked him, and leaned over and pressed butterfly-soft kisses to his bruises.

Shit. His cock went hard. It didn't care that he'd been beaten up, it just cared that Siv's mouth was on him. He didn't move as she kissed each mark. When was the last time anyone had kissed his hurts?

Usually, it was him patching up other people. His heart clenched. Damn, this woman—with her tough shell and big heart that she hid so well—was getting under his skin.

She sat back and stared at him for a moment, then rose. "I'm going to order some dinner. What do you feel like?"

"Um, Thai, if you like it."

She stilled. "I love Thai food."

"Make sure you get some pad thai. And I like a green curry."

"I love pad thai too." Siv pulled out her phone, wandering toward the windows as she placed the order.

Ryder decided to change. His jeans were covered in dirty alley muck. He rose, absorbing the throbs.

"What are you doing?" Siv demanded.

"I need to change."

Her mouth flattened. "I'll get some clothes for you. Stay there." She disappeared into the master bedroom where their bags were, and returned a moment later with gray sweatpants, a white T-shirt, and a small, brightly wrapped gift, with her name written on it.

She passed him the clothes then held up the box. "I found this at your place. What is it?"

"Clearly, it's a gift for you."

She stared at him like he'd just said he was from Mars. Hell, did no one spoil this woman?

She swallowed. "You don't have to—"

He grabbed her wrist. "I like getting you gifts. Go on, open it." He reached for the fastening of his jeans. "I'll change."

He expected her to turn, but he should've known better. He shoved his jeans down and she watched, her gaze lazily traveling down his body.

Annnnd his cock got even harder.

Siv could hardly miss it, tenting his boxer shorts. He awkwardly pulled the sweats on.

"Let me help you." She helped him pull his clean T-shirt on.

Hurting, he dropped onto the couch. Damn, he hated being weak.

"You're in pain." She sat beside him, still holding the gift.

"The painkillers will kick in soon. And I've had worse."

She raised a brow.

"On deployment. Got into a few scuffles. Worst was when I had badly injured soldiers to deal with, and insurgents attacked. We got out, but we were a little battered."

He'd lost two men. One had died before Ryder could help him. The other had died in Ryder's arms.

He still woke some nights, blood on his hands, hearing the death rattle in the man's chest.

"Hey. Ryder?" Siv touched his jaw. "Where did you go?"

"Afghanistan. The memories dull, but they never go away."

She nodded and he saw understanding in her blue eyes. "I lost a teammate once."

He grabbed her hand. "You were special forces."

She nodded. "I joined the Norwegian Army, but it wasn't long before I was flagged for Jegertroppen."

"What's that?"

"An all-female special forces unit."

"Really?"

"Really."

He held up a hand. "Give me a second. I'm imagining an entire team of badass females."

She shook her head. "After a couple of years, I moved to the main Forsvarets Spesialkommando, FSK. I loved it." She dragged in a breath. "But it isn't always easy."

"No, it's not. What happened?"

"We were on an oil rig. Terrorists had taken it over and had hostages. My team infiltrated to rescue the hostages and take control back."

"Didn't go to plan?" He threaded their fingers together.

"No." She gave a harsh laugh. "That's an understatement. One terrorist saw that they were losing and detonated explosives. I was tossed against some equipment. I had a concussion, broken ribs. I was pretty beaten up." She pulled in a breath. "My friend, Rolf..."

Ryder squeezed her fingers.

She gave him a sad smile. "Part of the platform tilted. He slid and I reached for him. I missed him by an inch. He didn't survive the fall off the platform."

"I'm sorry." She'd been hurt, concussed, but she'd still tried to save her friend. Typical Siv.

"Rolf had saved me on a previous mission. I was pinned down and out of ammunition. He broke cover to get to me. He saved my life."

"And that's how you should remember him. I know the guilt is always there. That you didn't try hard enough, didn't move fast enough, that you should have done something differently. Every patient I've ever lost, I never forget. I always wonder what I should've done differently."

"Ryder." Her face changed. "You save lives."

"Not always." He gave a final squeeze of her fingers and waved at the gift. "Open it."

She tore the wrapping off and opened the small rectangular box.

Then her chest hitched.

She pulled out the silver chain with a circular pendant on the end. The pendant was covered with an intricate design.

He nodded. "It's a—"

"Viking shield," she said.

He nodded. "I saw it in the window of this little shop

near my place, and knew it was perfect for you. Beautiful and badass."

She stared at him.

Ryder tried not to fidget. "The guy in the shop assured me that it was a Norwegian design. I hope he wasn't lying."

"It's beautiful, Ryder."

He smiled.

Then she moved and straddled his lap. She was careful not to bump his chest.

His pulse jumped and he gripped her hips. "Siv—"

Her mouth collided with his.

Damn. She kissed him hard, deep, and with a groan, he pressed his mouth closer and took control of the kiss.

She tasted like the best flavor—sweet, but spicy. He pulled her closer, need like fire in his gut, but bumped his injuries. He hissed.

"That's enough." She slid off him.

"*No*—"

"You got worked over today, Ryder. I'm going to make sure you rest."

He scowled.

Then she leaned over and bit his lip. "But once you're better, then I plan to fuck you, long and hard."

His aching cock throbbed, and he groaned. "You're trying to torture me."

She just smiled.

Ryder ignored the pain and tumbled her onto the couch.

"Ryder, your bruises!"

He braced himself over her. "I just want you to know

that you're mine, Siv. Soon, I'm claiming you. I'll taste and touch every inch of that fine, long body of yours. I'll make you come so many times, you'll be sobbing."

Her chest hitched. "*Ryder.*"

There was a chime at the door, and he let out a growl.

"That'll be dinner," she said.

He helped her up, but caught her hand one more time and squeezed her fingers. "You've been warned."

SIV ATE another mouthful of pad thai noodles. *Yum.* So good.

She eyed the TV and watched the NFL game. "No!"

"Your team is going down, my badass goddess."

She shot Ryder a look. He was sprawled on the other end of the couch, shoving a mountain of food in his mouth. The man must work out constantly to stay in such good shape.

"Or should I say *gudinna*." He waggled his eyebrows.

She fought back a smile. "I'm not your goddess."

"Yes, you are. How about *skatt*?"

Treasure. She wrinkled her nose.

He ate another mouthful of noodles. "I know. *Månestråle.*"

Moonbeam. She laughed, but deep down, she was touched he'd taken the time to learn the Norwegian words."

"No, it'll definitely be *honningblomst.*"

Honeyflower. She shook her head and forced herself to look back at the game. The man was just too tempting.

Her team wasn't having a great quarter. "My team looks tough and scrappy. They'll fight back." She was cheering on the San Francisco 49ers. It seemed right to support the team of her new home.

Ryder grunted and sipped his beer. They'd had several good-natured arguments over football in the last hour.

His cell phone rang and he grabbed it. Then he rolled his eyes. "One of my brothers ratted me out." He pressed the phone to his ear. "Hi, Mom." He paused. "I'm fine. A few bruises, that's all." Another pause. "Mom, I promise. I looked worse when Cam and I fought over that bicycle when I was in the fifth grade." He grinned. "You were so lucky to be blessed with three boys." He caught Siv's gaze and winked. "Mom, I'm helping Vander with a case, so I won't be home for a bit. Can you feed Crank for me?"

"Who's Crank?" Siv murmured.

"My cat doesn't hate just you, Mom. He hates everyone. It isn't personal."

Siv raised her brows. Ryder had a cat.

"Actually, I'm not alone. I'm working the case with a beautiful Norwegian lady Vander hired. She's former special forces and I'm trying my best to get her to date me."

Siv's eyes widened. She waved a hand at him. *What the hell was he doing?*

"Her name's Siv. I know, it's pretty, right? You'll love her, and absolutely, when we finish this case, I'll bring her over for dinner."

Siv shook her head.

"Will do, Mom. Love you."

Sagging back on the couch, Siv looked at the ceiling. It was pretty hard to resist a man who clearly adored his mother. "You shouldn't have told your mother I'd come for dinner."

"Now you have to come." He looked smug. Then when he shifted a few times, she realized he was uncomfortable.

"You need more pills?" She rose.

He gingerly touched his side. "Yeah, maybe."

She knew it wasn't good if he agreed so readily. She was surprised how much she hated seeing him hurt. She found the pills and the arnica cream that she'd bought from the pharmacy.

She strode back into the living room. The apartment was really great—she eyed the magnificent view—but a little too fancy for her.

"Here." She handed the pills over.

He took them and washed them down with some beer.

"Now, let's get that shirt off," she ordered.

He sent her a thousand-watt smile. "Babe, anytime you want me naked, you just have to ask."

Siv rolled her eyes and held up the tube of cream. "I'm putting this on your bruises."

"Arnica? Okay."

She nodded.

"I used to carry a few tubes when I was on tour. Good for bruises and swelling."

She sat beside him. "Yes. I use it as well. One time, a rope snapped when I was rappelling from a NH90 helo."

"Shit. You could've been killed."

"Thankfully, I was only six feet from the ground, but I landed on some rocks. Makes your bruises look puny." She helped him ease the shirt off.

Her chest locked, then her heart did a funny jerk. The man had a hell of a body. He was cut, and muscular. There was a smattering of light brown hair across his pecs. And those abs...

Focus on the bruising, Siv.

Ryder looked down and groaned. "I look like a toddler fingerpainted me with black paint."

Siv shifted closer and squeezed cream onto her fingers. "Sit back, and don't move."

He slouched on the cushions, and she smoothed cream along his collarbone. Her gaze traced over the ink on his shoulder and arm.

"I like your tattoo."

"Thanks."

She took in the overlapping scales, flourishes, and waves that she realized were fire. "It's a dragon." It was stylized, but the powerful creature was there, hidden in the art.

"Yes. In Asian tradition, the dragon symbolized wisdom, power, good fortune, and strength. I figured all those things were good for a guy in a war zone to have on his side." He smiled. "Plus I wanted something badass."

She wanted to trace the tattoo, but restrained herself. She already had her hands on his body and she didn't need more temptation. Squeezing out some more cream, she spread it along his rib cage.

"You're lucky they didn't break a rib." She gritted her

teeth, really wishing she could spend a few minutes with the assholes who'd attacked him.

Ryder made a sound. "Not for lack of trying."

Siv kept spreading more cream on, careful not to press too hard. He could've been killed. Her throat tightened. This man had been pushing her buttons since she'd met him, but a world without Ryder Morgan in it would be a much darker place.

She realized how much she fought not to smile or laugh around him. She smoothed the cream on the bruises on his abs, her fingers tracing the dips and ridges. His belly tightened under her touch. Her gaze dropped lower, and she saw the large bulge tenting his sweats.

Heat coiled in her belly and she looked up.

There was a faint flush of color along his cheeks. "Sorry, it gets like that anytime you're around."

Siv wanted to touch him, desperately.

"In fact," he continued. "I'm pretty sure I've been hard since the first time I saw you in that killer red dress." His lips curled. "You are so damn beautiful. Stunning."

Siv swallowed. "No one's said that before."

Ryder growled, pressing a hand over hers on his abs. "That fucking ex did a number on you, didn't he?"

"No. Maybe a little. I was in the military so long, so dressing up..." She shrugged. "I'm better with fatigues and boots."

Ryder smiled. "I bet you rock those, too."

"You have an answer for everything." She shook her head. "My father divorced my mother when I was young. Just after Inger died."

Ryder muttered a curse.

Her lips curled. "He deserves that. He is a bastard. He never looked back, barely saw or contacted me. When he did, it was to express his displeasure that I wasn't more...classy and feminine, as a good daughter should be. He really didn't like me joining the military."

Ryder's next curse was even more colorful and she found herself wanting to laugh. He just made everything lighter.

"You should have seen his face when I joined the FSK." She shook her head. "I don't dwell on it."

"You can't tell me that your asshole dad and your douchebag ex haven't colored how you look at things." He gave her a look.

"Maybe." The men in her life might have scarred her more than she liked to admit. She sighed. "My mother was so angry. For a long time, I blamed myself for him leaving. For not being good enough."

"Screw that, Siv. Your father is to blame for his actions."

"I know that now, but some things bury themselves deep."

"And then asshole boyfriends rub salt in the old wounds." Ryder cocked his head. "What happened with the asshole?"

"He didn't mind having a military girlfriend when I was away most of the time. Once I got out, we saw each other more often." She shrugged. "I realized I didn't like him as much as I thought. He was obsessed with his work, making money, making appearances with the right crowd."

"And you don't give a shit about that."

She shrugged a shoulder. "Then one night, I defended us against a drunk asshole, and Johan couldn't deal with it."

"Because he's an insecure idiot."

"We broke up. I found out he'd been cheating on me when he got engaged to another woman—a younger, elegant, well-connected woman—only six weeks after we ended things."

Ryder cupped her jaw. "It's his loss. Babe, watching you fight is a massive turn-on."

A laugh burst out of her. "Actually, I believe you when you say that now."

He waved a hand at his straining cock. "I have evidence that anything you do has an effect on me."

"So I see." She slid her hand down and palmed the thick bulge.

Ryder made a strangled sound. "Please tell me you've changed your mind about when we can have that hot, hard fuck."

"No. Not until you're better."

He groaned.

Siv tightened her hold on his cock. Oh, it felt very, very nice. "You're hurt. No sex tonight. I want to take care of you."

"You mean torture me," he said grumpily.

She slid her hand inside his sweats and wrapped her hand around his heated length. *Oh, God.* He was all hot, silky skin over rock hardness. She stroked him.

His hips jerked up. "Siv—"

"Just enjoy, Ryder." She pressed her mouth to his ear. "Don't move or jostle your injuries. Just feel."

She felt pre-come at the end of his cock and ran a finger through it. She explored every inch of that delicious hardness. She couldn't wait until she could do everything she wanted to it.

"Babe...Siv," his voice was guttural.

She pushed his sweats down and pumped his cock. Oh yes, it was a mighty fine one.

His hand covered hers, urging her to move faster.

Her gaze locked with his green one. They jacked him together, moving faster. It was one of the sexiest things she'd ever done.

Heat filled his cheeks. "Fuck, I'm going to blow."

"I want to watch."

With a deep groan, he came. His come spilled over his gut and their joined hands. She watched his face the entire time. Those handsome features were contorted with pleasure, his chest heaving.

Finally, he slumped back on the couch. "That was..."

"Sexy." She rose and headed into the bathroom.

She washed her hands, then found a washcloth and ran it under the water.

When she returned to the couch, she smiled. He hadn't moved. His now flaccid cock was still on display. He was fully comfortable with his body.

She cleaned him up, and felt him watching her. He pulled his sweats back into place.

"Siv." His quiet, and damn near reverent, voice got to her.

She let him tug her closer, and his lips touched hers. It was a deep kiss that she felt to her toes.

She was fighting a losing battle to stay away from this man.

A ringing cell phone made them part.

"It's mine," he muttered, reaching for it. "Morgan." He listened for a second, his face morphing granite-hard. "*What?*"

The barked word cracked through the room. Whatever it was, the news wasn't good.

"How many?" A pause. "*Fuck*. Shit, Santiago. Okay. Can you get the results for me? Yeah, thanks." He ended the call and exploded off the couch.

Siv felt rage throb off him. She rose slowly. "Ryder?"

"Fuck!" He kicked the coffee table and met her gaze. "Three more homeless people came into the clinic tonight. Two died of total organ failure. One is on life support."

"Oh, God." She pressed a closed fist against her chest. Those poor people.

Ryder gripped the back of his neck. "One was Scratch. He's dead."

Siv moved, pressing her hand to Ryder's arm. "I'm so sorry, Ryder."

"The fucking Fosters. These people had lives. Lives that were shitty enough without the Fosters interfering. They had *no* right to steal it from them."

She hugged him. "No, they didn't deserve to die. And we will stop the Fosters."

She felt Ryder's body tremble and knew he was at his limit—physically and emotionally. She took his hand and led him into the bedroom.

The master bedroom had the same white walls as the

rest of the apartment, but a circular mirror on the wall, and throws of gray and tan on the bed, softened the space.

He didn't say anything and she pulled him down on the bed. Once he was settled against the pillows, she climbed in beside him, fitting her body against his carefully so she didn't jostle his injuries. His arm clamped around her and he buried his face in her hair.

"Just hold on, Ryder," she murmured.

CHAPTER TWELVE

Ryder woke the next morning and took half a second to work out where he was.

This wasn't his bed.

And he didn't often have a long female body pressed into his back, legs tangled with his.

In a flash, he remembered their fake apartment and investigation into Chiron. He turned his head and the movement caused a few twinges that reminded him of yesterday's fight.

He looked down his body. The bruises weren't pretty, but he wasn't actually feeling too bad. Carefully, he shifted onto his back.

And watched Siv shift, snuggling into him.

Damn. He fingered her hair. She'd left it loose, and there was a lot of it. It was mostly brown but shot through with streaks of blonde.

Her face was pressed to his chest, and some of the toughness had leaked out of her features in her sleep. He let his gaze trace her high cheekbones. The long length of her pressed against him, did nothing to help his morning hard-on.

She stirred, then went still. Like he'd done, taking stock.

She lifted her gaze. "Good morning."

Her voice was husky with sleep.

"Morning, wifey. There are advantages to being fake married."

She sat up, eyeing his bruises. "How are you feeling?"

"Pretty good, considering." Except for the desire raging in his gut.

Her gaze locked on his hard cock, trapped by his black boxer shorts. She pulled in a breath. "I'll take the bathroom first."

He watched her slide off the bed and stalk across the room. Her pajamas were a large, well-washed T-shirt.

Damn, those legs were something. Ryder leaned back on the pillows. They had nothing to do today but wait to hear from Ace, and make an appearance outside as Ryan and Stella.

Ryder blew out a breath. Waiting sucked. It always felt better to take action. He'd felt the same on missions, where he preferred to be on the helo headed in to help, versus twiddling his thumbs at base.

Siv reappeared, her hair still loose, but brushed. She sat back on the bed, and he got a waft of minty smell that said she'd brushed her teeth.

Damn her no-sex ban. He wanted her more than he'd wanted anything or anyone ever before in his life.

"So, what have you got on under that?" He nodded at the shirt.

She plucked at it. "This? My secret."

He plumped up the pillow. This was...nice. Waking beside her and seeing that sleep-induced softness on her face. "We're married, you know. A wife shouldn't have secrets from her loving husband."

That got him an eye roll. "You seem to be moving well."

"I have two brothers. I know how to take a few hits."

She fiddled with the covers. "So, we just sit around and wait to hear from Ace?"

"Yeah."

She stretched her long legs out on the bed. The shirt rode up dangerously high, showing inches of silky skin.

His cock lengthened.

Unable to stop himself, he reached out and touched her smooth thigh.

Her gaze whipped up to his. "What are you doing?"

"We can't go out and be Siv and Ryder, and we can't do anything on the case until we hear from Ace. So, I'm seducing you."

Her lips parted. "I'm not the kind of woman to fall for seduction."

"Really?" He shot her a slow smile. "I bet I could prove you wrong." He slid his hand higher.

"Ryder, you're hurt..."

"I'm fine. A little dinged up, but I've been hurt worse." He found a scar on her leg and caressed it. "So how about if I try to seduce you? If I can, I get to do whatever I want to you."

Faint color filled her cheeks. "And if you can't?"

"I'll cook you breakfast." He gripped her thigh and felt her muscles flex.

"I don't think I can keep saying no to you," she murmured.

Elation hit him. "So don't."

"All right, but you should know that I've had training to withstand torture," she said.

"Oh, babe, I'm not going to torture you...much." Ryder moved fast. He gripped her thighs and yanked her toward him.

She fell on her back, letting out an expulsion of air.

"Now..." He slipped his fingers around the back of one of her knees, skating over her skin. "The skin here is so soft." He took his time stroking.

She watched him with a fascinating mix of desire and confusion on her face. It was fun sparring with Siv, and it was even more fun to keep her guessing and on her toes.

He slid his hands higher.

"Now I get to see what's under this shirt. I love the way it drapes over your breasts."

"Ryder."

"*Shh.*" He gripped the hem and pushed it up, uncovering inch after inch of sleek thigh.

Then he pushed higher, and his gut locked.

Fucking hell. His cock was so hard it hurt. She wasn't wearing any panties. And she was waxed bare.

"*Siv.*" His voice was choked.

"No one's ever looked at me like you do," she murmured.

"Get used to it." He slid his hand up to her sweet folds between her legs and stroked.

Siv gasped, her hips lifting.

"Already so wet for me, babe." Ryder felt desire growing, like a damn firebomb. "Now—" He gripped her, pushing her legs apart. Then he slid his hands under her toned ass and lifted her to his mouth.

"Oh...God," she choked out.

Sweet, sexy Siv. With long, dragging licks, he pulled in the taste of her. He wanted to memorize it and leave his marks on her. He scraped his stubble on her inner thigh and heard her gasp.

God, he loved going down on a woman and driving her out of her mind with pleasure. What he wanted right now was to give Siv that pleasure and hear his name on her lips.

She twisted, but he held her still. There was a flash in her eyes. She wasn't used to a lover being stronger than her.

Ryder went back to work, scraping his teeth over her clit.

"*Oh...*" Her next words came out in mangled Norwegian.

He closed his mouth over her, working her hard. She bucked, but he kept his mouth on her. He felt that strong body trembling for him. He slid a hand down and then thrust a finger inside her wet warmth.

"Ryder!" She jerked, her breathing turning choppy.

Damn, she was tight. He slid a second finger inside, stretching her.

"I want your scent all over me," he growled. "I want mine all over you."

Her chest hitched.

He thrust his fingers into her, and made her moan. "Mine." He'd never, ever been this possessive over a woman. "I want to come inside your sweet pussy every day. Mark you as mine."

He knew he was coming on strong. He'd never said things like this to a woman, but he couldn't stop himself.

Her lips parted. He closed his mouth over her clit, and watched and felt her orgasm hit. She screamed, her body bucking and jerking her against his mouth. He licked her through it until she lay there, panting and dazed.

"You're the most beautiful thing I've ever seen." He bundled her hair into his hand, tugging a little as he leaned over and pressed his mouth to hers.

This kiss was slower, but no less hot. Ryder kissed her deeply, losing himself when she kissed him back.

He knew that she tasted herself on his lips.

"Now, my Norwegian goddess." He bit her jaw. "Are you feeling seduced?"

Blue eyes met his. "I'd be lying if I said no." Her voice was husky.

He smiled. "That means I can do whatever I want to this delectable body."

She licked her lips. "I guess it does."

SIV'S BODY was still shuddering with small jolts of pleasure.

God. Ryder had known exactly what to do with his mouth, and exactly where to touch her.

She looked up into his handsome, sinful face. It was the sexy smile she noticed first, but it was the look of pure desire in his eyes that really took her breath away.

This man saw her. Wanted *her*. Her heart thumped. A part of her wanted to run.

But Siv had never run from a challenge in her life, and Ryder Morgan had earned her trust these last few days.

"So," she said, "what are you going to do to me?"

Heat flared in those sexy, green eyes. He shifted closer and winced.

Her gaze dropped to his bruised torso.

"I think you'll have to be on top, my sexy goddess."

She smiled. She liked the top.

Ryder settled his big body back on the pillows. Siv quickly pulled her shirt over her head, enjoying the look on his face as he took her in. Then her hands tangled with his as together they shoved his boxer shorts down. He kicked them away.

Her gaze went to his beautiful cock. It was long and thick and perfectly formed. She licked her lips.

"Getting some ideas of your own?" he murmured.

She climbed up the bed, stroking her hands up his muscular legs. It looked like he ran a lot, and spent a lot of time in the gym. Good, they could work out together. She moved between his legs and took hold of his cock.

Ryder groaned. "You want my cock, babe?"

"Yes." Everything inside her clenched tight.

"Then put your mouth on it, Siv. Drive me crazy."

She wrapped her lips around the swollen head of his cock. She listened to his groans as she licked and sucked.

She took her time, wanting to learn every line, vein, and ridge. He really had a gorgeous cock.

Ryder slid a hand into her hair. "Look at me, Siv."

With her lips still on him, she looked up that strong body, past the hard abs, sculpted chest, and strong throat to that face.

His green eyes were burning.

"If you keep going, I'll come," he said.

She gave him a suck, and his fingers twisted in her hair.

He grunted. "I want to come inside you, Siv. Come straddle me and sink down on my cock."

Siv's belly was a mass of electricity. She'd never wanted a man this much. She crawled higher, careful of his bruises.

He reached to the side table and pulled out a condom packet.

She tore it open and rolled it on. His hips jerked.

"Hurry up, Siv," he growled. "Or I'll come in your hands and not in your sweet pussy."

Biting her lip, she shifted her position. His cock brushed her folds, and one of his hands gripped her hip.

She sank down, sliding that thick, hard cock inside her.

They both groaned.

"I knew you'd feel so good," his voice was deep, gritty.

Siv leaned forward, taking every inch of him. She pressed her lips to his, then straightened and started to fuck him.

"So. Damn. Beautiful." Ryder's hand moved to her belly, then cupped her breast.

She picked up her rhythm. Oh, he was so deep. His hips bucked, filling her even more, but the timbre of his groans changed. From pleasure to pain. She stopped.

"*No*," he growled.

"That hurt you."

"Don't care." His fingers bit into her hip. "Keep riding me, Siv."

She lifted off him and heard him mutter a curse.

"I don't want you hurting." She considered the logistics. Then she turned and went down on her hands and knees in the center of the bed.

She lowered her cheek to the covers and looked back at him. "Let's try this way."

She saw his nostrils flare. His gaze skated over her upturned ass and she fought back a tremor of need.

Ryder rose to his knees and moved behind her.

"*Fuck*. So perfect." His hand stroked over her ass. "Strong but curved. Your skin is so soft." His fingers dipped between her legs and stroked. "All over."

She spread for him. Offering him all of her. Trusting him.

"I love you spread like this. For me."

Oh, God. She bit her lip.

"So wet for me." He pushed a finger inside her. "What do you need, my goddess?"

"I need you." Her voice was barely comprehensible. "I need your cock, Ryder."

"As you wish, babe."

He gripped her hips, then slammed inside her.

Siv's head flew back.

Perfect. *Brilliant*. Every inch of him filled her. She

moaned, her hands twisting in the sheets, searching for purchase.

"Fuck, Siv. You feel so damn good."

He drove into her, flesh slapping against flesh. Her body lurched under his steady thrusts. It was hard, sexy, fast. Everything inside of her shifted, raw, hot pleasure filling her.

She rocked her hips back against him, welcoming his thrusts.

"*Ryder*." His name was all she could manage. It came out as a plea, a demand.

One he answered.

"My sweet, sexy Siv. Taking my cock. Making me feel so damn much." He didn't slow his thrusts, but slid a hand under her and found her clit.

She cried out.

"You need me, just like I need you." His body covered hers. As he strummed her clit, his other hand gripped her shoulder for more leverage.

He claimed her. On the next hard thrust, Siv's staggering orgasm hit. She screamed again. That was twice, now. She'd never screamed for a man before Ryder.

Pleasure was a dazzling, breath-stealing rush.

"Fuck me," she cried. "Don't stop, Ryder." She was totally lost in the sensations, in the connection to this man.

With a snarl, he turned her head and his mouth took hers.

As he kissed her, another climax hit her, tossing her up again.

Then his deep, guttural cry filled her mouth. On his

next savage thrust, he stayed deep inside her as his body shuddered through his own release.

Siv's arms collapsed. She took Ryder's weight before he shifted to the side. He stayed pressed close to her.

"Fuck me." He sounded winded.

Siv smiled. "That was..."

"Brilliant. Awesome. Mind-blowing."

"I was going to say energetic, but those work, too."

Their faces were close together. He pressed a kiss to her nose.

Somehow, that was more intimate than everything they'd done before.

"You're a goddess, Siv." He stroked her damp shoulder. "My goddess. *Gudinna mi.*" He smiled. "Are you ready to do it again?"

Her eyes widened. "We'll kill each other."

His grin widened. "I couldn't think of a better way to go."

CHAPTER THIRTEEN

Ryder walked down the street, keeping an eye out for a tail.

He slid an arm across her shoulders and pulled her close. When she leaned into him, he felt a pleasant kick in his gut.

They were headed to the coffee shop, acting as Ryan and Stella, for anyone who was watching.

God, he really liked this. She was tall, and a perfect fit against him.

A perfect fit in bed, too.

They hadn't slept much. They'd gotten creative to avoid his injuries. Shit, he was getting hard at just the memory of sliding into her tight warmth.

A pinch on his side jolted him back to reality. Siv was looking up at him.

"Are you listening to me?"

"Yes."

"You are not. You're thinking about sex."

He raised his brows. "How did you know?"

Her lips twitched. "You get this look on your face, and you're half hard." She moved her hip, brushing against him. He stifled a groan and pinned her to his side. "You're right." He nipped the shell of her ear and lowered his voice. "I was thinking about how good it feels to slide inside you, and the sound you make when—"

"*Ryder*." Color hit her cheeks.

He loved that he could make this tough, ex-special forces soldier blush.

He kissed her. He could kiss her all day long. He bit her lip. "We should keep kissing a bit longer, you know, in case someone's watching."

"Just for the job?" She slid her hands into his hair.

She clearly liked his hair. She'd spent a lot of the night with her hands buried in it. She kissed him this time, doing it thoroughly.

"Do you think Ryan and Stella still kiss like this?" she murmured. "After years together?"

"My sexy goddess, I'll kiss you like this forever."

He saw the flash of shock in her eyes.

Hell, Ryder had never truly considered the concept of forever with a woman. Maybe he'd given it a few thoughts after watching his friends at Norcross, and Hunt, fall in love and claim their women. But he'd been sure it wasn't for him.

Until he'd laid eyes on Siv, and his world had tilted off its axis.

He cupped her cheeks. Realization washed through him.

She was *his*. He was going to stake his claim and

make her his. And not just for a few weeks or months. He just needed to bring her around to the idea first.

"Come on. Ryan needs coffee."

They set off, holding hands. The local coffee shop was busy. All the tables were full, and there was a short line at the counter.

"What do you want?" he asked.

"Latte with an extra shot."

"I'm on it."

He joined the line while Siv stood near the window. She grabbed a discarded newspaper, looking at it idly, but he knew she was studying the street through the window.

Ryder ordered and checked his phone. He had a bunch of text messages from Ace. The man was wading through data he'd pulled off the Foster's lab system, but his search was taking time.

Maybe Ryder and Siv could help Ace to speed things up. They needed a lead, and Ryder wanted it now, not in days. They needed to find out where the hell the siblings were manufacturing their drug.

"We'll get them, Robbie," Ryder whispered. "I promise you."

Ryder got the coffees and dumped some extra sugar in his.

"Hi, there."

He lifted his head. A small blonde with a reed-slim body and a wide smile stood beside him in yoga gear.

"Hi," he said.

She held out a napkin. "I've been watching you since you came in. I wanted to give you my number, in case you're interested in going out some time."

"Well, that's mighty friendly, but I'm taken."

The woman stepped close enough for him to smell her perfume. She stuck the napkin in his pocket. "Just in case you decide you aren't taken."

Over the blonde's shoulder, he saw Siv spot the woman. Her gaze narrowed.

"Well, I should warn you that my woman is kind of possessive. And mean."

The blonde's smile widened. "Well, I'm sweet." She touched her tongue to her lips. "And I'm not possessive. In fact, I have a friend and she's a gorgeous brunette. We like to have fun together."

Ryder raised a brow. "As much fun as that sounds..." He saw Siv making her way toward them. "I have to decline. My woman is more than enough for me."

His Norwegian goddess arrived.

"I can't take you anywhere." Siv shoved her hands on his hips.

"I was just standing here, getting a coffee." He held her coffee cup out to her.

She took it, looking exasperated. She snatched the napkin out of his pocket and turned to the blonde.

"He's mine." She stared at the woman until the blonde started to look nervous.

"I was—"

Siv stuffed the napkin in the woman's coffee cup. "Run along."

The blonde hesitated.

"Now," Siv said.

The woman turned and hurried away.

Grinning, Ryder sipped his coffee.

"You're a menace." She shook her head. "You're too hot, and too charming."

"It's my cross to bear, and now it's yours." He slid an arm across her shoulders as they headed outside. "Did you spot any surveillance?" He kept his voice low.

She shook her head.

"Let's get back, I want—" His cell phone rang. "It's Ace." Ryder pressed the phone to his ear. "Hey, man."

"Ryder." The tech man sounded serious.

"You've got something?"

"I do. First, it looks like the Fosters' security team has stopped digging on you two. I suggest you keep up your married-couple persona a bit longer, but I think you're in the clear."

"Okay, we'll stay at the apartment for now. We need a lead, Ace. I was thinking we could help you with combing through the data."

"I might have a lead for you."

Siv was watching Ryder's face and he held her gaze.

"Go on," he said.

"I ran a search on the medical examiner's office, since you said they blew off Robbie's autopsy."

There was no one around on the sidewalk, so Ryder moved close to Siv. "I'm putting you on speaker, Ace. Siv's here."

"Hi, Siv," Ace said. "The chief medical examiner is new. He's rebuilding the office after some scandals."

"What scandals?" Siv asked.

"A backlog of autopsies, the office being too slow to issue death certificates, missing narcotics."

Ryder frowned. "I heard the office lost their certification last year."

"Yes. The new guy, Dr. Michael Atherton, is shaking things up. He sacked a few of the assistant medical examiners, hired a few new ones, and told the others to clean up their game. He's solid."

"But a few of the old guard might not be, and might be open to bribes," Ryder said.

"Ding, ding, ding," Ace said. "Including Dr. Stephen Hyland. He's a few years away from retirement, a chronic gambler with a love of fishing, and has three ex-wives. He was reprimanded by Atherton, but kept on in the department."

"And?" Siv prompted.

"And he did Robbie's autopsy, and he's doing the new people who died of organ failure. Added to that, he just purchased a very expensive new boat."

Ryder sucked in a breath, heat trickling into his veins.

"One he can't afford," Ace added.

"The Fosters paid him off," Ryder said.

"I'm running the money trail, but there's a tangle of companies involved. It'll take some time to track it."

Ryder met Siv's gaze. "I think we should pay Dr. Hyland a visit."

"I concur."

SIV DROVE the X6 toward the Office of the Chief Medical Examiner in Bayview, south of the city.

"Hunt lives out this way." Ryder was sprawled in the

passenger seat, but she didn't think for a second that he was as relaxed as he looked.

"What's the plan?" she asked.

"We go in as relatives, clearly distraught over our loved one's death. Ace is messaging me a list of autopsies that Hyland has on his books." He lifted his phone. "We're checking in about our dear brother Aaron."

"One of the new homeless who died?"

He nodded.

"Did you know him?"

"No." Ryder looked out the window.

She stared at his face. But he'd known Robbie and Scratch. He'd stand for them all, give them a voice.

Soon, she pulled up at the modern, glass building that housed the Office of the Chief Medical Examiner. There was a fancy, abstract metal sculpture out front.

They headed inside. A young woman sat at the reception desk.

"I'll get us in," Ryder said. "You'll be in charge of sweet-talking Hyland."

Ryder sauntered toward the desk. The woman was young, maybe late-twenties, with her black hair cut in a cute pixie style. As she watched him get closer, her eyes widened.

Siv saw him unleash the smile. The receptionist was toast.

Siv hung back. She watched the woman blush as Ryder charmed her.

Funny how Siv saw through it now. Oh, Ryder Morgan had charm, no doubt, but he used it like a weapon or a shield. He kept things easy and fun, and didn't let many people beneath.

To the real Ryder.

But he'd let her.

Her pulse skipped. She saw the woman pick up the phone, smiling. Ryder glanced back at Siv and winked.

Okay, she wasn't totally immune to that charm. Especially now she knew exactly how good he was in bed. How talented he was with his hands, mouth, cock.

Heat stirred in her belly. Dritt, *not now, Siv.*

Ryder strode back. "We're in. Hyland's down in the lab."

The receptionist led them to a door. "Just follow the signs to Autopsy One."

"Thanks, Aimee." Ryder smiled.

Siv watched Aimee stare at him, blushing.

"Come on, darling brother." Siv shoved him ahead of her.

"Sure thing, my lovely sister."

Siv snorted. Their footsteps echoed on the tile floor. "I think you'll feature in Aimee's dreams tonight, Morgan."

He tugged on her hair. "As long as I'm in yours is all I care about."

They reached double doors marked Autopsy One. The doors opened and a technician pushing a gurney with a sheet-covered body on it, passed through.

Ryder and Siv stepped against the wall and let the man pass.

They entered the lab. There were three workbenches, all made of stainless steel. One was empty. Two were covered in shrouded bodies.

A man in a lab coat stood at the back of the room, tapping on a computer.

Siv unbuttoned the top two buttons of her shirt and let her ponytail down. Ryder watched, raising an eyebrow.

She winked and shook her hair out. Then she stepped forward. "Dr. Hyland?"

The assistant medical examiner turned, a frown on his face. He was in his sixties, with a large nose, and thinning, salt-and-pepper hair. He had the florid look of someone who drank too much.

"I'm Steve Hyland." His gaze dismissed Ryder and settled on Siv. He smiled.

She smiled back, keeping it a little solemn. "Thank you for seeing us. I'm Sarah. I wanted to ask about my poor brother." She let out a sad sigh. "He'd been on the streets for several years. We tried to help him." She fluttered her hands. "We tried everything."

"I'm sorry." Hyland's face settled into sympathetic lines, although his gaze did a quick dip to her cleavage. "What was your brother's name?"

"Aaron," Ryder said. "Aaron Mullen."

Hyland nodded and moved back to the computer. "I'm sorry, Sarah. Drug use took its toll on your brother's body and caused his death."

Siv cocked her head. "But he didn't use drugs."

"I'm sure you had no idea what he got involved with on the streets. It's a dangerous place, with drugs everywhere."

"Then perhaps we should talk about your new fishing boat, Dr. Hyland." Her voice took on a silky purr.

The man stiffened. "What? Who are you?"

Ryder stepped up behind Siv. "People looking for answers. Answers for the people being used and killed by the Fosters and their company, Chiron."

There was a flare of panic in Hyland's eyes. "Fosters? Chiron? Never heard of them."

Siv leaned against the empty bench. "I think you have. I think we'll eventually trace the juicy big payment you've received back to Christian and Caroline Foster."

Ryder stepped closer and Hyland stumbled into a workbench, sending a few things rattling.

"Now talk," Ryder said.

Hyland shook his head, spluttering. "I've nothing to say. I have no idea what you're talking about."

"We're talking about wealthy, unscrupulous entrepreneurs taking advantage of disadvantaged, vulnerable people on the streets. Testing drugs on them illegally."

"No." Hyland shook his head. "These people died of their addictions to illegal substances."

"They did not," Ryder roared.

"I suggest you quit lying, Hyland," Siv said. "We want confirmation that the Fosters asked you to cover up these deaths."

Hyland swallowed convulsively. "I don't—"

"Stop lying!" Ryder thumped his fist on the bench.

Hyland jumped.

Siv touched a hand to Ryder's chest, felt the tension thrumming through him.

Hyland looked away blew out a breath. "If I talk, I'm dead."

"This is a chance for you to step up and do the right thing," Siv said.

The man's face twisted. "What do you care? They were just homeless trash. The dregs of—"

Ryder surged forward, gripped Hyland's throat and slammed him against the wall.

The assistant medical examiner spluttered and clawed at Ryder's hand.

"They were people," Ryder spat. "They were living, breathing people. They had demons, like we all do, but they laughed and cried and had friends, and they mattered."

Hyland made a gurgling sound.

Siv grabbed Ryder's arm. "Hey, let him go."

Ryder's face twisted.

"It's okay, Ryder. We're going to get justice for them. We won't stop until we do."

Finally, he released Hyland. The man staggered and dropped into an office chair, rubbing his throat.

Siv swung around to face Ryder. "You all right?"

His mouth flattened. "They were all more people I couldn't save." His gaze dropped to the shrouded bodies on the benches beside them.

Her heart clenched. She saw the pain reflected in his eyes. His own demons.

"You can't save everyone," she said. "That's not your job."

He closed his eyes.

She wrapped her arms around him. "I'm here. Just hold on."

His arms clamped onto her, hard. She held on tight, offering what comfort she could. She heard the air shudder out of him. Then a chair squeaked, and she turned to face Hyland.

The man froze. "Get out, or I'll call security."

"You made some bad choices, Hyland," she said.

The man cleared his throat. "I didn't kill them."

"Maybe not, but you helped the people who did."

Ryder made an angry sound and Siv grabbed his hand.

"If you talk about our visit, we'll come back," she said.

Hyland stayed silent.

"You don't want me to come back," Siv warned.

She might walk out of here today, but soon, she'd happily hand over information on the man to the police and let them deal with him.

She dragged Ryder out.

CHAPTER FOURTEEN

Back in their borrowed apartment, Ryder stalked the main living area, gut churning.

That *asshole.*

Hyland had talked about Robbie and the others like they were worthless, nothing. Ryder kicked the coffee table and sent it skidding across the floor, but it didn't make him feel better.

He put his hands on the back of his neck.

How many more people would die before he worked this out? How many more people would he fail?

"Ryder?"

He turned. Siv stood watching him, her face covered with concern.

"I don't know how to help you," she said.

He shook his head. He felt like he was holding back a tide of shitty emotion.

"Fuck," he roared. He *hated* this helpless feeling most of all.

"Ryder, stop." Siv grabbed his wrists and he met her

blue gaze. "It's going to be all right," she whispered. "It'll take time, but you'll get there. We'll get there together, starting with nailing the Fosters to the wall. Then we'll shine a spotlight on this entire, ugly situation."

He sucked in some deep breaths. More than anything, he wanted those smug siblings who thought they were better than everyone else, to pay.

Ryder yanked Siv to his chest. She clamped her arms around him.

"That's it. Just hold on."

He buried his face in her hair and held on. "Dammit to hell."

"It's okay. Or it will be eventually. We'll make sure of it."

His Siv didn't crumble. She charged through, trying to find a solution. He stroked his hands up her back.

"Do you want to be alone?" she asked quietly.

His arms tightened on her. "No."

"I can—"

He lifted his head. "No."

He slammed his mouth down on hers. The kiss was fast and furious. She kissed him back, moaning in the back of her throat.

"Need you," he murmured.

He did. His head was filled with Siv, pushing out everything else.

"*Ryder*." Her tongue stroked his.

He backed her up, hands tearing open her belt and jeans. She helped him, kicking her jeans and panties free. Her shirt followed, leaving her in the most delicate, blue-lace bra. He loved the sexy things she wore under her clothes almost as much as he loved the body inside them. He flicked one nipple through the lace and watched it harden.

She made a needy sound, desire bright in her eyes.

He backed her up another step, until the back of her knees hit the couch. She sat down.

Ryder dropped to his knees in front of her and pushed her toned legs apart.

"You're so damn beautiful, Siv." Desire beat inside him. "Every time I look at you, touch you, I feel like I've done something right to be worthy of you."

Her face softened. "Ryder—"

"Every time." He stroked between her legs, and the look on her face—desire and need for him—made his gut clench. "Need to be inside you, Siv."

"*Yes*."

He fumbled with his pants and got his cock free. It took him seconds to pull a condom out of his wallet and get it on.

Then Ryder leaned forward and pressed the head of his cock to her.

"Ryder," she panted.

He slid inside her warmth, watching her body take him. "*Fuck* me." He absorbed the feel of her.

She moaned.

He pulled out, sank back in. He pressed his thumb to her clit, circling it as he picked up the speed of his thrusts.

"Yes." She moaned. "*God*. Faster."

He lost himself in the sweet oblivion of her. He kept working her clit, listening to her throaty cries.

"Ryder, I'm close."

"Good, babe. I want to feel you come." Her fingers wrapped around his wrist, holding him to her. Their gazes locked. *Damn.* There was nothing sexier than moving inside her while they watched each other.

Then she moaned, and her back and neck arched.

He watched her come, long and hard, as he kept rubbing her clit, his cock deep inside her tight body.

With difficulty, Ryder locked down his own molten need. "Want you to come again."

"I can't," she panted, still shaking with pleasure.

"Yes." He thrust harder, thumb still on her swollen clit.

Her second climax hit hard and fast. She cried out, body clamping down on his cock.

He couldn't hold back any longer. He surged up, slamming inside her. Buried deep, he came, grunting as pleasure obliterated everything.

Ryder found the strength to sit on the floor and pulled a limp Siv off the couch onto his lap.

"Too heavy," she mumbled.

"Hardly. Want you right here." He tucked her close.

"Your injuries—"

"It's fine if you don't move."

She relaxed against him.

"I like you close." He nuzzled her hair. "Thanks, Siv."

"It was a real hardship to let you fuck me to two orgasms," she said dryly.

He grunted. "It was more than that, and I needed it. Needed you."

"You're welcome, Ryder," she said softly.

They stayed there, snuggling, for a while.

"You ready to get to work?" she asked. "We aren't going to stop the Stepford siblings sitting around naked."

"Shame about that." He cupped her jaw, tilted her face, and kissed her. "I'm sorry to see you cover that magnificent body of yours, but yes, let's get to work."

They cleaned up and dressed, then ended up at the dining table, with both of their laptops. Siv made coffee and snacks.

"Ace sent through part of the property data for us to look at." She sipped her black coffee.

"I thought you liked lattes?"

"I like coffee in all its varieties." She ate some pieces of apple and almonds that she'd put on a plate. "In fact, Norway has the second highest per capita coffee consumption in the world after Finland."

"Really? Guess you have to keep warm up that way."

"I'll make *kokekaffe* for you some time. It's a special Norwegian steeped coffee. It's best brewed over a campfire when you're on a hike. Then we call it *turkaffe* or hiking coffee."

Ryder sipped his coffee "You like hiking?"

"Love it."

"I'll take you to Mount Tamalpais State Park one weekend. It's one of my favorite places to hike. There are over two hundred miles of trails stretching all the way to the Pacific. It's got everything, from forests to ocean views to rolling hills."

Her gaze met his for a beat. "It sounds great. And I'll make you *turkaffe*."

"And I'll find a secluded spot to get you naked and have my wicked way with you."

She laughed.

Sipping their coffee, they got back to work on the data.

"These are the least likely properties to hold the lab," Ryder said.

"Right. Ace is combing through the more promising ones."

"Guess it pays to double check."

They clicked and tapped. Ryder liked working with her. Liked the silence, and the small sounds she made when she was thinking.

"Man, these two own a shitload of things," he muttered.

"Why risk it all by carrying out illegal drug testing?" she said. "It threatens their entire business."

"There's definitely something wrong with the drug," he said.

Siv shook her head. "It still doesn't make sense. If word got out that Trelaskin wasn't as great as they'd hoped, sure, the company stocks would take a hit, but why risk your entire business by breaking the law?"

"We'll work it out," he promised. We won't stop until we do."

GOD, this was boring.

Siv clicked through more property data. There were

investment apartments, a house in Napa, commercial properties.

What there wasn't, was anything that showed signs of housing a lab.

She glanced at Ryder, and her heart thumped. He was so damn handsome. His hair was down, almost brushing his shoulders. He hit the keyboard, his brow furrowed.

"Anything?" she asked.

He grunted. "No. A whole lot of no."

"It's important we check everything." She rose. "More coffee?"

"I'll take a soda. Any more coffee, and I won't sleep for a week."

It was late afternoon, the day slowly giving way to night. She grabbed them both sodas and dropped back into her chair. Her computer chimed and Ace's lean face appeared in the window. The man was looking a little haggard.

"Hi, Ace," she said.

"Hi." He ran a hand over his hair.

"You look tired, my man." Ryder leaned in.

Ace sighed. "I am. Maggie's not sleeping well at night."

Ace's fiancée was due to have their baby soon. Ryder nodded. "Hard for her to get comfortable?"

"Yeah, add that to scouring through every detail of the Fosters' life, and I'm dragging. I'm glad you guys are helping."

"We haven't found anything," Ryder said.

"Well, I found some interesting facts on the dynamic duo," Ace said.

Siv and Ryder straightened.

"Really?" she said.

"Chiron is teetering on shaky ground," Ace said.

Siv frowned. "What? I thought they were worth billions. Chiron's loved by everyone, right? The stock price is up. And they sell other drugs."

"A few of their other drugs haven't quite been as successful as hoped. And R&D is expensive. The Fosters are up to their eyeballs in debt."

"But they own a butt load of properties." Ryder waved a hand at his laptop screen.

"The *bank* owns a butt load of properties. Christian and Caroline have huge debts. They're billionaires on paper alone, all due to the shares of Chiron."

"And if Chiron's stock prices fall..." Siv sat back in her chair.

Ace nodded. "They lose everything."

"And everything hinges on their wonder drug, Trelaskin," Ryder said.

Ace lifted a finger. "Correct. I uncovered some hastily hidden reports. A study by an independent doctor who said Trelaskin doesn't work. That the early test results were overstated."

Siv gasped. "If Trelaskin doesn't work..."

The Fosters would have nothing.

"This explains why the fancy lab is empty," Ryder said.

Ace nodded. "If they know they wouldn't get

approval to move to human trials, then they aren't going to waste money on staff in their lab."

"Which the market is waiting on," Siv added. "They have investors handing over a lot of money..."

"And if anyone got wind of it, Chiron goes bust." Ryder cursed. "But they still think they can make it work."

Siv met his gaze. "So, they're running illegal human trials. Trying to perfect the drug."

"Fuckers," Ryder spat.

"We still need to find the lab," Ace said. "When I find something, I'll let you know."

"Thanks, Ace," Siv said.

Ace ran a hand over his face. "I'm heading home, but I'll keep the searches running. I'll talk to you tomorrow."

"We'll keep looking, too," she said. "Night, Ace."

Ryder huffed out a breath. "We should probably take a break too. Order some dinner." His lips quirk. "What does my lovely wife want to eat?"

Siv looked back at the computers. "I want to check a few more things—"

There was a knock at the front door.

They both rose. No one had called up to be buzzed into the building.

Siv met his gaze, then moved into the entryway. She checked the peep hole on the front door and straightened. Swinging it open unveiled four women.

She'd met them all since she'd started work at Norcross Security. The bombshell blonde in the fitted, navy-blue dress was Harlow Carlson, Easton's fiancée. The pretty, slender brunette in the cream, lace dress topped with a fitted, black jacket was Rhys' woman, Haven McKinney. The slim blonde in leggings and a large, white shirt with pale-blonde, curly hair in a messy bun on top of her head was Savannah Cole, Hunter Morgan's fiancée. The short brunette in front in the statement-red pantsuit and holding a huge designer handbag was Gia Norcross.

"What are you four doing here?" Ryder growled. "Siv and I are undercover."

"We know." Gia strode in, the other women following. "We heard you guys are happily married." She smiled. "We came to see if Siv had murdered you yet."

Ryder crossed his arms over his chest. "You came to be nosy. If the bad guys spotted you—"

Gia waved a hand, her engagement ring glinting. "Oh, please. You know who my brothers are. Our cover story is that I'm meeting an important client who lives on the tenth floor. And we came in the back entrance."

"I'm guessing your men don't know you're here," Ryder said.

Gia tossed her dark curls over her shoulder and headed for the kitchen. "They aren't the boss of us."

Savannah shrugged. "I protested about coming, but Gia made me. She's small, but bossy."

"I'm organized and confident," Gia countered.

"And a bit scary," Savannah added.

Ryder shook his head. "You're going to be in trouble."

"Ryder." Haven's face fell. "You're all bruised." She crossed to him and touched the side of his face.

"A run-in with some thugs. I'm fine."

"You're sure?" Harlow leaned in and hugged him.

Siv saw him wince, but he hugged the woman back. Savannah touched his arm, her worry clear.

"Siv's taking good care of me," he said.

All the women's gazes swung her way.

"Really?" A smile flirted on Harlow's lips.

Ryder grinned. "*Really* good care."

Siv made a sound. "Why don't you just tell them we're sleeping together?"

"Because there isn't much sleeping going on."

Savannah started laughing, while Harlow clapped her hands together. Gia and Haven were smiling.

Gia dumped her huge handbag on the kitchen counter and pulled out a bottle of tequila, a cocktail shaker, and other ingredients. "This calls for margaritas."

Ryder's eyebrows flew up. "Do you have an entire bar in that bag?"

Gia ignored him. "Siv, since we can't take you out for cocktails, and ply you with questions about Ryder, we brought the cocktails to you."

Ryder shook his head.

A loud knock thumped on the front door.

Siv raised her brows, while Ryder strode over. When he checked the peep hole, he fought back a laugh.

This time, it was Vander, Saxon, Easton, Rhys, Hunter, and Cam.

Saxon strode in. "Contessa, I told you *not* to come here." He waved a hand. "This has your name written all over it."

Gia sniffed. "I don't take orders from you, Saxon Buchanan."

His gaze narrowed. "You do sometimes."

"You could have compromised Ryder and Siv's cover," Vander said.

"No one saw us, and we used a cover story." Gia propped a hand on her hip. "We aren't stupid."

Vander looked like he wanted to yell.

Brynn appeared in the still-open doorway, carrying an armload of pizza boxes. "Sorry I'm late. Someone help me with these. I got pizza from Tony's."

Vander eyed his woman and shook his head. He then went to help her carry the boxes in.

Cam lifted the beers he was holding. "Who wants a drink?"

Siv watched the men all claim their women for quick kisses. She saw Hunt Morgan tug on Savannah's hair, and murmur something to her. The detective looked a lot like Ryder, but a more clean-cut, big brother version.

Soon, she found herself on the couch beside Ryder, who'd slung an arm around her shoulders, eating excellent pizza and sipping a very good margarita.

"So, Ryder's infamous charm won Siv over." Gia sat perched on an armchair, Saxon sitting at her feet. "We weren't sure which way things would go."

Siv froze and glanced at Vander. She hadn't been quite ready to announce to everyone that she and Ryder were, whatever they were. Vander's face looked as impassive as always, but he was a hard man to read.

"Damn," Cam muttered. "That means Vander takes out the betting pool."

Siv lowered her drink. "You guys were betting on when Ryder and I would...?"

"When you'd take pity on him," Cam said. "I bet against him."

"What?" Ryder shot his brother the finger.

"He kind of wore me down," Siv said.

That got chuckles out of everyone.

"And I think my charm actually worked against me." He smiled at her. "Luckily, I have other good qualities."

Siv acted surprised. "You do?"

He pinched her side.

The conversation drifted. The group talked a little about the case, but she noted the Norcross men kept it light and didn't go into detail. The women talked about their work, upcoming weddings, Sofie and Rome attending an event in Mexico City, and Maggie and Ace's impending new arrival.

Siv sat there, listening to Ryder's deep laughter as he absently stroked the back of her neck, and watched the group. They included her without a thought, and she realized how much fun she was having. These were good people. Many of them were very wealthy—her gaze moved to where Harlow sat on Easton's lap—but they were all so down-to-earth. They didn't care about making appearances or doing the right thing or being seen at the right places. They were just themselves, and they accepted her as part of the gang, just as she was.

They cared about each other. She listened to Ryder and Cam argue about football. This group was a team. It made her realize how much she missed her team from the FSK. It was nice to belong somewhere again.

Finally, Vander rose. "Well, we'd better call it a night."

Everyone started moving and packing things away.

Her boss met Siv's gaze. "Ace briefed me earlier. He said you're searching for the Foster's lab."

She nodded. "We haven't found it yet, but we'll keep at it. Tomorrow, Ryder and I won't stop until we find where they're making the drug."

Brynn appeared at Vander's side, her face serious. "As soon as you get definitive proof, Hunt and I want the information. I want to be a part of bringing these assholes down."

Vander slid his arm around his woman. "Don't worry, Detective, you'll get your chance."

Soon, the apartment emptied out. Siv closed the front door.

"Had fun?" Ryder was leaning back on the kitchen counter.

"I like your friends and your brothers."

"They like you back, and I'm pretty sure you just got inducted into the gang." He smiled, slow and sexy. "Are you ready for bed, Ms. Pedersen?"

Heat flared, curling low in her belly. "I think I am, Mr. Morgan."

Her case would be there, waiting, in the morning. But right now, she had a hot, sexy medic she wanted to play with.

CHAPTER FIFTEEN

Siv tightened her hands on Ryder's broad shoulders, the tiles cool behind her back. She moaned, feeling her orgasm swelling, bearing down on her.

He gripped her hips, driving his cock inside her as the water washed over them.

"Get there, Siv," he growled.

"*Harder*," she panted.

His mouth took hers and she felt the edge of his teeth. His powerful body kept thrusting in her and she knew she was about to come.

"God," she breathed against his mouth.

"Come, babe. *Come*."

She was full of him, his cock stretching her, and sensation crashed over her. She cried out, feeling everything inside her body spasming.

"Fuck, I can feel you coming on my cock."

Siv gripped him, her eyes closing as she rode the wave of intense pleasure. The world contracted to just her and Ryder.

Then she felt his next heavy thrust. He kept his cock buried deep as he grunted through his climax, jetting inside her.

She dragged in a shuddering breath, pressing her face to his wet hair. She pressed her lips to his temple, tasting his skin. She breathed him in, the essence of Ryder. She listened to the sound of his deep, uneven breaths, then trailed her hand across his shoulder.

He made a sound, his mouth finding hers.

"Morning shower sex with my wife rocks," he said.

She shivered. "No complaints here."

Ryder finally set her down, then slapped her ass. "I'll deal with this condom, then make coffee. I'm guessing you want some."

"You guessed right."

She watched through the glass as he swiped a towel across his sculpted chest, then wrapped the towel around his lean hips. He sauntered out of the bathroom.

Siv dipped her head under the water. She was getting in way too deep with him. All her defenses were long gone. Whatever Ryder wanted, she'd have a hard time telling him no.

The case comes first, Siv. Deal with Trelaskin and the Fosters, then worry about your love life after.

Just the thought of the L word had her flicking off the shower and getting out.

Whatever happened, she knew she could trust Ryder. If he was done with her, he wouldn't lie or cheat, he'd tell her. Her heart squeezed.

Work. She had to get to work.

Two hours later, she was sitting at the table with a now-cold mug of half-finished coffee and a stiff neck.

Siv clicked on a picture of Christian and Caroline's Palo Alto estate. It was gorgeous—lots of natural stone, and valley views. The article was a spread for some magazine, and the glossy pair were posing inside the huge, renovated kitchen.

"Look at this place," Siv muttered.

Ryder frowned at the polished photos. "Isn't it weird that two adult siblings live together?"

"Yes. And in such a big place. The estate is thirteen acres and costs a cool fifty million."

"Nice."

"Fraud pays." Siv clicked through some photos. One showed Caroline in a lab coat.

Siv froze.

The woman was leaning against a gleaming, stainless-steel workbench.

"Wait. This is a picture of Caroline in an area that it says she's outfitting as a private lab. She says 'I still like to get my hands dirty. I love the challenge of creating drugs that can help and heal and save lives.'"

Ryder stiffened. "Shit, they have a lab in their home."

"I saw renovation invoices for the place somewhere." Siv tapped madly. "I glanced over them yesterday."

The first lot of invoices was for the kitchen renovation. There was one for flooring. Landscaping.

Then she saw it.

"Ryder, *look*." She pointed at the screen. There were invoices for lab workbenches, fridges, lab equipment, a high-tech sprinkler system.

He made a sound. "They have a lab in the basement of their fucking house."

Siv scanned the invoices again. "It definitely looks like it."

He clicked the keyboard, then swiveled. "Look at this article."

It showed Caroline, younger, less polished. She was grinning. She was in a lab and holding a test tube.

"Lab work was her thing," Siv said.

"She could be doing the work on Trelaskin herself."

"They need it to work, or they lose everything." Siv turned. "We need to get into their Palo Alto estate."

Ryder yanked her in for a quick kiss. "I'll make more coffee and then let's make a plan."

A few moments later, he brought up all the information they had on the estate.

"They have a lot of cameras." Ryder tapped a finger on the table. "Security guards, but the place they're using doesn't have a great reputation. The guards have no prior skills, and are only given a five-week training course."

"Let's call Vander and Ace." Siv made the call.

Moments later, her boss, Ace, and Saxon appeared on screen.

"We found the Foster's lab," she told them.

Ace leaned forward. "Where?"

"At their home. The fancy Palo Alto estate. They had a lab put in the basement during renovations."

Ace eyes widened. "Makes sense. Nice work."

Siv inclined her head and looked at Vander. "They have some security, but Ryder tells me the guards aren't from a top-notch outfit."

"Arma Services," Ryder said.

"They're not a top-notch anything," Vander agreed.

"Pulling up the camera system now." Ace clicked on his tablet. "Mediocre system and easy to crack."

"Any cameras in the lab?" Siv asked.

The tech guru shook his head. He lifted his tablet and tapped. "Looks like the Fosters are out today. They're scheduled to attend a luncheon at Stanford."

"Siv, Ryder, we'll meet you at the estate," Vander said. "You two will need to make sure you don't have a tail."

"We think they've lost interest, but I'll make sure of it," Siv said.

"All right," Vander said. "We'll bring gear. See you soon."

As soon as the call ended, Ryder rose. She felt his tension and it made her nervous.

"You can't lose it," she said. "You have to stick to the plan."

He gave her a curt nod. "I've got my anger locked down." He blew out a breath. "This is it. I can feel it. We'll finally get all the details on how Robbie died. And make the Fosters pay."

Siv gripped his arms. "Yes, but you need to stay focused. Don't let the emotions drive you." She didn't want to see him get hurt.

He gave her a lopsided smile. "Worried about me, my Norwegian flower?"

She rolled her eyes, but she was. This man had worked his way deep under her skin. He meant something to her.

Ryder cupped her cheek. "I promised not to go off half-cocked, Siv." He stroked her skin. "We're going to stop Trelaskin from hurting anyone else, and make sure the Fosters end up behind bars. Then we'll come home and celebrate. Naked. With a bottle of something."

She smiled. "Do you ever not think about sex?"

He kissed her. "Not since I saw you stalking across the dance floor."

Her heart flip-flopped. The look of desire on his face scorched her, but she watched him close it down. His face turned serious, and she saw the courageous medic who'd gone into combat so many times to save others.

A man who would risk it all for a homeless veteran who'd been his friend.

The man Siv was falling for.

She locked her feelings down and dragged air into her tight chest. She needed to follow her own advice, and not let her emotions drive her.

She needed to keep Ryder safe, and get the job done.

SIV DROVE THEIR COVER CAR—A sweet, little Mercedes C class registered to Stella Peters. They pulled out onto the street, and Ryder discreetly scanned around and checked the mirrors.

No sign of a tail.

Clearly the Fosters had decided that Ryan and Stella were legit investors.

"I'll drive around a bit, then head to Palo Alto," Siv said.

They were both wearing cargo pants and T-shirts. Ready to sneak into the Foster's estate.

Ryder looked in the side mirror and frowned. "Change lanes."

Siv didn't hesitate or question, just shifted lanes. He watched the silver sedan three cars back do the same.

"You see them?" he said.

She checked the rearview mirror. "I see them." She smiled. "But we won't for long."

She took the next corner fast and Ryder was pushed back in his seat. She didn't make it obvious that they were onto their tail. She didn't break the speed limit, but she showed her skills as she took several more turns, changed lanes, and drove them through a narrow alley.

"Do you see them?" she said.

"Hell, no. Because my woman is a badass, and can lose a tail in her sleep."

She glanced at him. "Your woman?"

"Yep. You got a problem with that?"

She rolled her eyes. "So cocky."

"I think you like my cockiness." He winked.

Siv laughed. God, he loved that sound. He wanted to make her laugh more often.

It was a sound he wanted to listen to for the rest of his life.

His hands clenched. *Shit.* She was it for him. He wanted to marry her, put babies in her belly one day, if she wanted them. He wanted to sleep beside her, make love with her, hear her laugh every day. He was in love with Siv Pedersen. Of course, he was.

Ryder swallowed. *Focus.* For now, Robbie needed

him, but when this job was over, he was going to spend some time convincing Siv Pedersen to take a chance on him.

He was going to make her happy.

They hit the highway south, then finally reached Palo Alto. Instead of heading into the city, they veered west toward the hills.

"The Foster's estate is in Portola Valley," he said. "A thirty-two-thousand-square-foot residence with mountain and valley views."

Siv followed the directions to the meeting place, and found two X6s waiting for them on a small, tree-lined, side road. Saxon, Rhys, Cam, and Vander stood by the vehicles. The men were all in black cargos, with black ballistic vests pulled over their shirts.

Siv pulled up. Ryder got out and nodded at the men. He gave his brother a fist bump.

"Good work, you two." Vander handed over vests and weapons.

As Siv pulled her vest on and checked her Glock 19, Ryder fought not to get hard. Yes, his woman being a badass did it for him.

He pulled his own vest on and tightened it, feeling a faint twinge from his bruises. He checked his Glock and then slid it into the holster on his belt.

He looked at Vander. "What's the plan?"

"We'll work in pairs. Go in, incapacitate any guards." He held out a box containing small earpieces. "Ace will provide comms and shut down the cameras. We're just having a look around to find the lab. Don't kill anyone."

Ryder slipped his earpiece in.

"Cameras will be down in one minute," Ace's voice said in his ear. "You have two guards. One by the gate, one inside, somewhere."

"Acknowledged," Vander replied. "We'll avoid the one at the front by coming in from the eastern side of the estate, where the house is close to the boundary fence." He scanned the group. "Saxon and I will secure and search outside. Cam and Rhys will do the upper level of the house. Ryder and Siv will do the lower level. Call if you need assistance. Ready?"

They all nodded.

They headed down the side road, breaking off and heading into the trees.

Ryder slung an arm around Siv's shoulders. "This is fun. And I'm totally getting the hang of this looking like a couple thing."

Siv rolled her eyes.

"I like it," he murmured.

Her gaze flew to his.

He had to kiss her, and hated that he had to keep it quick. He savored her lips for a brief second.

She elbowed him. "Mind on the job—" her voice lowered "—until later."

"Now, that is good incentive to get this job done. I want later, Siv. A lot of later."

She gave him one long look before facing ahead.

They reached the imposing stone fence. He watched Siv run and jump, then pull herself over the stone wall. Ryder followed, leaping off and landing in a crouch.

Vander and the others had disappeared. All four of the men had been Ghost Ops, and they were damn spooky when it came to sneaking around. He knew they could handle themselves.

"This way," Siv murmured.

They darted across a well-groomed, green lawn. The house was stunning. Architecturally designed, it was a sprawling mass of stone and stucco.

They moved onto a spacious patio, and Siv nodded her head toward some sliding-glass doors. They were unlocked and opened soundlessly.

There was no one inside the large living area. It was all wood and cream tones, with wooden ceilings overhead with chunky wood beams, wood floors, and a huge stone fireplace.

"Nice digs," Ryder muttered.

"Let's find the stairs to the lower level." Siv moved inside without a sound.

She crept ahead of him, toward a wide hall.

Ryder followed. He saw a flash of movement to his left and spied a dark-haired woman in a maid uniform, a pile of folded towels in her hands.

Hell, Siv wouldn't see her at that angle. If the woman took a few more steps, she'd spot them.

He dropped to the floor and yanked Siv down.

To her credit, she didn't fight him or make a sound. He pointed, and pressed a finger to his lips.

They crawled behind the large, cream couch, and he pressed up against her.

He peeked around the corner and saw the maid walk past, humming to herself.

The woman's footsteps faded away.

Siv nodded, and they rose. They moved cautiously

down the hall. He spotted the staircase ahead, and she pointed.

They headed down quickly. Siv held up a closed fist, and they listened.

"No sign of the interior guard on the upper floor," Rhys murmured in the earpiece.

Shit. That meant the guard was still unaccounted for.

Siv moved slowly, sticking close to the wall.

The next level opened into a large, recreational area, with a U-shaped couch and huge TV. There was an air-hockey table off to the side. Ryder peered in some of the doors opening off the room, and noted they were all guestrooms.

They kept moving. The house was huge. Ahead, glass doors opened into a covered courtyard with a glass-ceiling. It was filled with lush, green plants, and a comfortable seating area.

Just past that was an indoor lap pool. He knew there was also a large pool and outdoor entertaining area upstairs. This one was for exercise, with a well-equipped gym attached.

Where the hell was the lab? Shit, he hoped they weren't wrong. Maybe the Fosters had moved it?

They passed through the gym, just as the door on the other side of the room opened.

Hell. His pulse spiked. They had nowhere to hide.

A suit-clad guard stepped in. He looked about Ryder's age, with russet-red hair.

The man saw them, frowned. "Who the hell are you, and how did you get down here?"

Siv smiled. "Oh, I'm a friend of Caroline's. She invited us."

The guard stepped toward them, his frown deepening. "There's no one on the list today."

"Oh, I guess she forgot—"

The guard's gaze dropped to Siv's vest and Glock. He whipped his own weapon up. "Get on the ground. Now!"

Siv let out a breath. "All right, we'll do this your way."

She moved like lightning and kicked the gun out of the man's hand.

Ryder rushed in and punched the guy. The guard fell over a weight bench, and Siv crouched and touched the man's neck. Whatever nerve point she hit, it only took seconds for the guy to sag.

She yanked out some zip ties, then bound and gagged the man.

"You look hot doing that," Ryder said.

He watched her fight a smile, and rise. "Come on, let's hide him, and keep searching."

CAUTIOUSLY OPENING THE DOOR, Siv slipped out of the gym and into the corridor.

Ryder was right behind her. He moved that big body well, staying silent.

The guard was now tied up in a storage cupboard in the gym.

She scanned the hall. This one was more utilitarian. Her instincts pinged. No homey, designer décor here.

She waved at Ryder, and he nodded. They moved toward the door at the end of the hallway.

Siv slowly cracked it open and looked inside. There was no sound or movement, so she pushed it open.

Bingo.

The lab wasn't big, but unlike the one she and Ryder had checked out in the industrial area, this one was clearly in use.

The workbenches were covered with equipment, notepads, computers, vials filled with liquid.

She walked in, scanning for occupants.

No one.

She walked along one of the workbenches, then looked up at the glass-fronted fridges. The shelves inside were stocked with vials, filled with clear fluid.

"See what you can make of this," she said.

Ryder nodded, face focused. He leaned over and touched a computer, the screen flared to life. He started typing.

"Vander?" Siv touched her ear. "Vander, are you there?" There was no response. "Ace? This is Siv."

Silence.

She cursed. "Something's interfering with the comms."

Ryder didn't look up from scanning the data on the screen. "Then let's get what we need, and get out of here, fast." He froze.

"Ryder?" She moved closer.

"It's all here." He met her gaze, anger raw and hot in his eyes. "Caroline's been working on Trelaskin here. It failed early tests, and she felt she needed human data to perfect it." His jaw tightened. "Even though she didn't know if it would be safe, she found her own test subjects."

Siv's pulse jumped. It was pure evil. Testing an unknown, potentially dangerous drug on vulnerable people.

Ryder tapped the keyboard. "All her fucking notes are here. She's kept meticulous details." He sucked in a sharp breath. "Fuck, she bribed a person running a nursing home."

Siv's gut curdled. "She tested the drugs on the elderly?"

He nodded. "Some died. But it was blamed on their old age, or other medical conditions. But Caroline needed younger, healthier test subjects. It's all outlined here neatly. The fucking *witch*." He turned and swiped an arm across the bench, knocking things to the floor. A glass beaker shattered.

"Ryder." Siv grabbed his arm.

"She decided to target the homeless. To offer them money. She needed the healthiest of them." Ryder turned back to the screen and hissed. "Jacko's name is here."

Siv took a second to place the name. "The nurse from the clinic?"

"The bastard sold Caroline medical records of the healthiest homeless people that came through the clinic."

"No," Siv breathed.

Ryder tapped furiously. "Here are the records. She knew it wasn't working, and people were dying, but she kept doing it."

Siv pressed against him, felt his pain.

Then she saw the name at the same time he did.

Thomas Robert Wilcox, test subject 25.

"Robbie was one of her guinea pigs." Ryder's voice was wooden. "He had no idea that he'd signed his death warrant. She killed him. For what?"

"So he could save the world."

The female voice had them both spinning around.

Caroline stepped into the lab, closed the door behind her, and locked it with a loud click.

The woman wore slim, black pants, a black shirt, and a lab coat. Her hair was up in an artfully messy knot that Siv figured the woman had probably spent a lot of time perfecting.

"You're a murderer," Ryder growled.

"No, I'm a savior. I'll cure cancer and save *millions* of lives. Stop endless suffering."

"You're deluded," Siv said. "Your drug is a failure, and you've killed people."

Caroline's elegant face moved into sympathetic lines. Did the woman practice that in the mirror?

"To achieve greatness, risks must be taken. Sacrifices must be made."

Ryder lurched forward and Siv grabbed him.

"Then you risk *yourself*, not others," he spat. "Why don't you put your damn drug in your own arm?

Caroline's face twisted. "I never meant for anyone to die. I just needed more time to perfect—"

"I've seen your data, Caroline." Ryder stabbed a finger at the computer. "Your drug is junk. It's a failure that kills."

The woman looked away and sniffed. "The only

people who died were really old or homeless. No one cares."

Siv had to yank Ryder back. He growled again.

"I care," he said. "You killed a good man. He didn't have some stellar career, and he wasn't a tech billionaire, but he was a good man. Although you aren't a billionaire either, are you? You're just a fraud and a failure."

Caroline stiffened and her mouth flattened.

Ryder continued, "Robbie wasn't rich, but he was decent. People cared about him, and he cared about others. And I'll make you pay for killing him."

Fear flashed through Caroline's eyes. "I *will* fix Trelaskin. It will change the world—"

"It's over, Caroline," Siv said. "Chiron will go bust, and you and your brother will go to jail."

The woman's eyes widened. "No. *No.* I'm a genius. I'm—"

"A fraud." Ryder shook his head. "People will remember Robbie and the others you killed, and in a few years, you'll be nothing. You'll be locked in a cell, just an ugly, cautionary tale to Silicon Valley."

Caroline's chest rose and fell fast. Panic was rising, and there were red spots in her cheeks. "Who are you two? Christian thought something was off about you both. He had you investigated."

"We know," Ryder said. "We've been putting on a show for your investigator."

Siv shifted, watching Caroline carefully. The woman wasn't trained, but cornered, desperate people could be dangerous.

"I'm Siv Pedersen, from Norcross Security and Investigations. This is Ryder Morgan, a medic and friend of Thomas Robert Wilcox. Mr. Wilcox's family hired us to find his killer. He may have lived on the streets, but he was a veteran and well loved by his brother Peter."

"Peter Wilcox." Caroline looked stricken. "I've met him. His brother lived on the street...?"

"Robbie was a vet with PTSD," Ryder said. "But his family hadn't abandoned him. He wasn't trash."

"They were all supposed to be nobodies," she whispered.

Disgust flared on Ryder's face. "It shouldn't matter if they had a wealthy family or not, they were people. What is wrong with you?"

Caroline straightened. "I never meant for anyone to die."

"Well, they did, and you're responsible."

She swallowed. "I can't go to jail."

Siv made a scoffing sound. "It's too late."

"Not if you never tell anyone." Caroline licked her lips. "I can make this lab disappear." Her gaze narrowed. "And you two as well."

Siv laughed. "You're going to take us on?" She shook her head. "We aren't vulnerable homeless people, and we aren't alone. Others know what you've done."

A strange, panicked look crossed the woman's face. "*No*. If I make you go away, it will all go away. I can work on Trelaskin until it's a success. I'll change the world."

Siv saw Ryder tense.

Caroline grabbed some jars of fluid off the bench. She lifted her chin. "I can't let you leave. I can't let you ruin my life's work."

She threw the jars.

Shit. Siv dodged. She slammed into a bench and one of the jars landed close by, shattering. The liquid sizzled, as it ate into the metal of the bench.

Dritt. It was some sort of acid.

CHAPTER SIXTEEN

D*ammit*. Ryder saw the acid burn into the metal of the workbench.

If that hit Siv...

Not that his woman looked worried. She lunged at Caroline.

The scientist threw another jar. Siv battered it aside and it hit the wall. Caroline dodged behind the workbench, and Siv followed.

"It's over, Caroline," Siv said.

"No! I'm destined for greatness, for success. I'm making the world a better place."

Ryder's jaw tightened. The selfish, entitled woman believed every word she said.

"You've made it worse." Siv darted forward.

With a cry, Caroline scrambled around another bench. "*No*."

"Yes. You've killed people. Lied to your investors and stolen their money. You're scum."

Caroline's face was white, her hair becoming askew.

She yanked open a fridge, pulling out vials. "I can't let you ruin me and Christian."

"It's not about you anymore," Ryder said, edging closer. "It's about justice for the people you killed."

"Just stand down, Caroline," Siv said. "Make it easier on yourself."

Caroline shook her head wildly. Her hair tumbled loose from its knot. "I'm a genius. I'm one of the youngest tech billionaires in the country. I'm going to change—"

Fuck. Her deluded beliefs were too ingrained.

Caroline snatched up a syringe off the workbench and jabbed the needle into one of the vials. She backed up.

Ryder frowned, and saw Siv do the same.

"Caroline, put that down," Ryder said.

The woman was breathing fast. "This is Trelaskin. A highly concentrated dose. You'll both die quickly. I'm sorry."

Ryder whipped his Glock up. "Put it down." Damn, Siv was too close.

Then Siv attacked.

She kicked Caroline, and the woman bent over, making a pained sound. Siv's next kick was to the scientist's arm. The syringe flew into the air and hit the tiles.

Siv followed through with two punches. Caroline hit a workbench, groaning. She was no match for Siv.

Siv yanked out some zip ties. "It's over—"

With a wild cry, Caroline grabbed a small centrifuge off the bench and swung the piece of equipment at Siv.

She managed to clock Siv in the jaw. While Siv was

surprised, Caroline leaped on her, and both women crashed to the floor.

Shit. "Siv!" Ryder circled the bench.

"I've got it," Siv said. "Give me a second."

The women wrestled. Siv ended up on top, pinning Caroline on her belly to the tiles.

The scientist surged forward, reaching out. Siv pressed a knee into the woman's back.

And that's when Ryder saw what Caroline was reaching for.

The dropped syringe of Trelaskin.

Heart knocking into his ribs, Ryder tried to get a clear shot. "Siv, watch out!"

Caroline grabbed the syringe and made a stab at Siv. Siv rolled off her.

Dammit. Ryder still didn't have a clean shot. He couldn't risk hitting Siv.

The women wrestled again.

"Drop the syringe, Caroline." Ryder advanced. The women didn't even hear him.

Siv rolled again. With an angry sound, Caroline lunged.

The syringe slammed into Siv's arm.

No.

Siv grabbed for it, while Caroline reared up. Panic filling his chest, Ryder fired, the gunshot echoing loudly in the lab.

The bullet clipped Caroline's arm. She screamed and it spun her away from Siv.

"Get down on the ground," he roared. "Now!"

Caroline stumbled, then tripped over a stool.

Ryder watched as the woman fell with a sharp cry. The back of her head hit the corner of the workbench, and she collapsed to the floor.

He rushed to Siv. She sat up and yanked the syringe free.

"Siv. *Fuck.*" He dropped to his knees, his heart pounding like a drum.

She threw the syringe to the floor and grabbed his hand. "It's okay. She didn't depress it."

His gaze dropped and he saw that the syringe was still full of fluid. He released a sharp breath.

"Thank God." He yanked her to his chest. The idea of losing her...

Siv kissed his jaw, then stiffened. "Oh, shit."

Ryder looked back and his gut clenched. Caroline hadn't moved. She lay on her side, her sightless eyes open. There was blood on the tiles underneath her head.

"Aw, hell." He moved to the woman and checked her pulse. The bullet had grazed her arm, but the blow to her head had killed her.

He was full of mixed emotions. Any death was bad. Even knowing everything she'd done—that she was responsible for Robbie's death, the death of others, and not to mention that she'd tried to kill Siv—it still didn't sit right.

A hand pressed to his shoulder, and he looked up at Siv.

"It's not your fault," she said.

"I know, but I wanted her in jail, not this."

"Come on. We need to get comms back and contact the others."

With a nod, he rose.

Suddenly, the lab door opened. "Caro, why was the door locked? Are you—?"

Christian Foster jerked to a stop, staring at them. He was in jeans and, no surprise, a black turtleneck. "What the hell are you two doing here?"

Ryder stepped forward, the gun pressed to the side of his leg. "Foster—"

But Christian surged forward and saw the gun. Then his gaze dropped to his sister's body.

Shock, anger, and grief rippled over his features. "Caro... No."

"I'm sorry," Siv said. "We—"

"You killed her!" The words were a harsh whisper. Christian's face twisted. "*Caro.*"

Ryder dragged in a breath. "It was an accident."

Christian's gaze went flat. "You aren't investors. I knew something was wrong with you."

"We're investigating your sham drug and the people you killed," Ryder said.

Christian shoved his hands into his hair. "They were all nobodies. No one cared that they died. Caroline was beautiful, accomplished—" His face twisted.

"They mattered, too, and no one deserves to be murdered," Ryder said.

Blazing eyes met his. "Yet you killed my sister."

"She attacked us first. I shot at her in self-defense, and she fell."

Christian shook his head. "You'll pay."

"Enough." Siv stepped forward. "It's over. We don't want anyone else to get hurt."

The man made an enraged sound, spun, and ran for the door.

"Stop!" Ryder yelled.

Christian slapped a hand to the wall and the lights went out. An alarm started blaring.

Shit. Ryder couldn't see anything. "Siv?"

"I can't see him."

Water spurted from the sprinklers on the ceiling, drenching them.

Dammit. A sudden shove sent Ryder sliding. He slammed into the workbench and fell. He heard a scuffle.

"Siv!" He pushed to his feet.

The door opened and slammed closed.

Fucking hell. Ryder leaped up and found the wall. He moved his hands, looking for the light switch.

"Siv!" he roared.

There was no answer. Pulse racing, he found the door and tried the handle. It was locked from the outside.

He kept moving and found the light switch.

He turned the lights back on.

Except for Ryder, and Caroline's dead body, the drenched lab was empty.

Foster had Siv.

No. *Fuck, no.* He turned and hammered on the door.

UGH, why did she feel so groggy?

Siv fought through the fog in her head. Her body was bobbing weirdly up and down. Did she have a big night? She usually didn't drink enough to have a hangover.

She managed to crack one eye open.

Someone was carrying her. She was draped over some guy's shoulder.

Thoughts tried to break through, but she couldn't put everything together. It was all a confusing jumble. She blinked slowly. Her clothes were wet. She lifted her head saw they were in a garage. She saw a row of expensive cars. Then she spotted the stun gun on the man's belt.

Stun gun.

Everything rushed back in.

Robbie Wilcox. The Fosters. Ryder.

Hell, Caroline was dead. And in the sprinkler-soaked darkness, Christian Foster had gotten the jump on her and stunned her.

Was Ryder okay?

She tried to get a handle on her worry. Right now, she needed to get free. And unfortunately, her extremities still felt tingly and numb.

The world whirled and she was dumped in the passenger seat of a vehicle.

Siv blinked.

"Ah, you're waking up." Christian jerked on her hands and tied them together with some rope. She blinked, trying to clear the blurriness from her vision. She'd shaken off stun gun affects before.

But this felt different.

"I drugged you," he said.

She flicked her gaze up.

Christian's face was a horrible mask. "Sedative. To keep you docile." He slammed the door and circled the sleek, red car.

She realized it was a Tesla roadster. The interior was almost futuristic, with sleek, cream seats, a small, curved steering wheel that looked like it belonged on a spaceship, and a glossy, rectangular screen in the center of the dash.

He got in, gripped the wheel, and the vehicle rolled out of the garage silently. The garage door ahead slid upward.

He was tense, looking around as they exited the garage. Then he gunned down the long, tree-lined driveway.

As they sped away, Siv saw two men running out of the house in the side mirror. It looked like Vander and Saxon.

"Caroline—" Christian's voice cracked, his hands flexing on the wheel. "That asshole killed her."

"Where is he?" Her voice was raspy.

"I locked him in the lab." Christian glanced at her. His face was grim, his eyes burning. "I wanted to kill him, but this is better. He took something important from me, so I'll take something important from him."

Her heart sped up. "He's...not really my husband."

"I saw the way he watched you. You matter."

Siv's breath hitched. "No, I—"

Christian made a sound. "He yelled your name. We'll see how he feels now that I've got what he cares about."

"Foster—"

"Shut up." He sped up, swerving a little on the road.

Siv felt aches reverberate through her body and stifled a groan. Her brain and body felt sluggish from whatever he'd given her.

"You committed fraud and murder," she said. "Trelaskin doesn't work. It kills. What happened to Caroline was—"

"I said *shut up*." He hit the highway and headed toward the city.

"Where are we going?" She lifted her bound hands to her face. Damn, he'd obviously found her earpiece, as it was gone.

"I don't know yet." He slammed a hand on the wheel. "All I can think about is my sister. She's gone." Sorrow drenched his voice.

Siv swallowed. "I'm sorry."

A muscle in his jaw flexed. "You will be, and so will your man."

She dragged in a breath. Ryder and the others would find her. Right now, she needed to stay calm, and wait for a moment to overpower Christian.

But she couldn't help but hope the others didn't take too long.

One thing she knew in her heart was that Ryder would come for her.

PANIC WAS hot in his veins. Ryder hammered on the locked door of the lab.

That fucker Foster had Siv.

Ryder knew she could handle herself, but when you were head over heels in love with someone, nothing stopped the worry.

His heart thumped. He *couldn't* lose her.

"Ryder?" Vander's voice came through the door.

"In here!"

He heard two muffled gunshots, and the door swung over.

Vander stepped into the doorway. He noted the sprinklers, and Caroline's dead body. "*Fuck.*"

"She fell and hit her head." Ryder charged out, flicking his wet hair out of his face. A grim-faced Cam stood in the hallway.

"You all right?" His brother asked, handgun clutched in his hands.

"Fine. Christian Foster has Siv."

Vander cursed and touched his ear. "Ace, I need eyes on Foster's car. He has Siv."

A muscle ticked at the edge of Ryder's eyes. "He must've incapacitated her."

"We saw his car speed out," Vander said.

"Rhys and Saxon are outside. Let's move." Vander touched his ear again. "And Ace, call Hunt. We have one dead body. Caroline Foster."

Ryder tried to get a grip on his emotions. Fear was riding him hard. "Foster might hurt her."

"She's made of tough stuff," Vander said.

Yeah, but she had soft spots too. She'd trusted Ryder enough to show the softness she kept hidden.

"Dammit." He shoved his hands in his hair. "Not knowing if she's hurt..."

"I've accessed security footage," Ace said. "Foster used a stun gun on her and looks like he injected her with something."

Ryder's pulse went crazy. He hoped to hell it wasn't Trelaskin.

"It looked like she was coming around in the garage," Ace continued.

Ryder blew out a harsh breath. Cam clapped a hand on his arm and squeezed.

Outside, they jogged through the trees and scaled the fence, headed for the X6s.

"We *have* to get them." Ryder dug deep, trying to find some calm. "Foster saw his sister was dead, and he lost it."

Vander's jaw tightened.

"And he knows that we're onto Chiron."

"He's got nothing left to lose," Saxon said.

Ryder's gut hardened. He needed to get to Siv before Foster imploded.

They reached the SUVs and Ryder flew into the passenger seat. Vander gunned the engine and sped off. The other X6 fell in behind them.

Then Vander touched the dash. "Talk to me, Ace."

"Okay, I've had a couple of glimpses of Foster's Tesla roadster. He's heading back into the city."

"Where is he taking her?" Ryder muttered to himself.

"Acknowledged, Ace," Vander said. "We're en route. Keep us posted."

"Can you see if she's okay?" Ryder asked.

"She's conscious," Ace said. "We're going to get her, Ryder. And knowing our girl, she'll have dealt with Foster herself by the time you get there."

Ryder's hand clenched into a fist. He sure as hell hoped so. But until they had Siv back safely, until he could hold her himself, he wouldn't stop worrying.

"It's going to be all right," Vander said.

"Hell, is this how you felt when that biker gang took

Brynn?" And it must've been how Hunt felt when his woman Savannah had faced off with her stalker. Like his insides were being torn out.

"Does it feel like you swallowed motor oil?" Vander said.

"Yeah," Ryder agreed.

"Then, yes."

Ryder blew out a breath.

"Keep it together," Vander ordered. "For Siv."

Ryder nodded. "Can you go any faster?"

With a half smile, Vander sped up.

CHAPTER SEVENTEEN

Siv kept trying to loosen the ropes around her wrists without her captor noticing.

They were back in San Francisco, but Foster showed no sign of slowing down.

"Where are we going?" she demanded.

"Be quiet." He reflexively clutched the steering wheel.

"You don't have a plan, do you?" She lowered her voice. "Do the right thing, Christian. It's over. Man up and—"

"Quiet! This is all your fault. If you and that guy hadn't come poking around..."

"People were *dead*. Their families wanted answers."

Foster cursed. "Caro and I were going to change the world."

"You're deluded."

He growled and sped up more, dodging through traffic when he could. Ahead, she saw the greenery of the Presidio. She'd been planning to visit the park as soon as she had some time off work. In the distance, she saw a glimpse of the Golden Gate Bridge.

"Where are we going?" she asked again.

She got no answer.

They drove through some short tunnels on the approach to the bridge. Siv looked in the side mirror.

And glimpsed a black X6 behind them, staying back several car lengths.

Her heart jumped in her throat. Ryder and her team were coming.

The red towers of the bridge rose up ahead. Foster sped up, zipping wildly through the traffic.

"You need to slow down," she said.

"I don't care what you think. You helped take the most important thing in my world away." His face twisted. "My life is over, and so is yours."

Her pulse jumped. He'd lost it.

He accelerated and they drove onto the bridge. Siv took a second to look out across the water. Suddenly, Foster jerked the wheel to overtake a car ahead of them. He clipped the car, and the other sedan screeched to a halt, turning in a half circle. Siv looked back and saw another car crash into it.

Behind them, she saw cars stopping...

Except two X6s that sped around the crash.

"Slow down," she tried again.

Foster laughed. "Maybe I'll crash us right off the bridge and into the Bay."

She kept her face blank. She continued working on the ropes, and felt them loosen and drop to the floor. She glanced out the window. She was pretty sure the bridge's red metal railings would hold even if he crashed them into it.

Ahead, she saw flashing lights. Her chest tightened. The police had set out a barricade on the northern end of the bridge.

Foster saw them and cursed. He skidded to a stop.

"Caroline wouldn't want you dead, Christian," Siv said slowly.

His mouth flattened into a line. "She wouldn't want me in jail, either."

"A good person takes responsibility for their actions." She thought of Ryder. He was a good man who still thought of all the people he'd lost under his care, still felt that he'd failed when he'd done everything he could and more.

Christian owned up to nothing. Ryder took on too much.

God, she loved him.

Siv bit her lip. She was falling in love with Ryder Morgan.

The Norcross SUVs screeched to a halt behind them. The men spilled out.

Vander was in the lead, striding forward. Then she saw Ryder. His hair was wet, gun in his hand.

Coming for her.

He'd never want to fight her battles, but he'd always want to help. He'd always support her as she did what she did best.

He'd never turn away from her, and always be there.

All of a sudden, Foster whipped a gun up, pointing it

at her across the interior of the car. With a lurch, she realized it was her Glock.

Shit. He stared through the windshield to the police barricade. Even from a distance, Siv made out Hunt's tall form. Then Foster looked back at the Norcross men.

He aimed the gun at Siv's head. "We're getting out."

"Okay, I'll—"

He roughly grabbed her shirt and yanked her toward his door. The console hit her hip, but she didn't argue with the man with the gun.

He climbed out and pulled her with him. He shoved her ahead of him, and jammed the gun into her back.

"Put down the weapon, Foster." Vander's voice was icy cold.

"*No.*" Foster shook his head. His gaze zeroed in on Ryder. "No, *he* has to pay for killing my sister." He shoved Siv. "A life for a life."

She looked at Ryder. His body was tense, his mouth a flat line.

She met his gaze.

I've got this. She tried to communicate it to him.

He jerked his chin.

Warmth filled her chest. Her man trusted her to do what needed to be done.

"Walk!" Foster barked.

They reached the railing separating the road from the pedestrian pathway.

"Climb."

Siv swung her legs over and saw some cyclists had stopped several feet away, watching the drama anxiously.

The wind ruffled her hair. The Bay and the San

Francisco skyline spread out before her. She'd take the time to admire the view, if it weren't for the gun pressed to her spine.

Foster climbed over, careful to keep her between him and the Norcross men.

He dragged her to the outer railing. The water below was blue, with little whitecaps caused by the wind.

She watched Foster's face go pale. It was a long way down, but nothing Siv wasn't used to from her oil rig work.

"Walk." He dragged her backward, and raised his voice. "Stay back or she gets a bullet in the back."

The Norcross men froze. She saw anger and fear blazing in Ryder's eyes.

They reached a spot where some maintenance was occurring on the bridge. There was white plastic draped over the railings, and some temporary signs and heavy toolboxes.

"There's nowhere to go, Christian." She kept her voice calm, steady. "You're stuck between the police and Norcross. It's time to put the gun down."

"No." He shook her. "I can't go back. Caroline's gone." Raw pain shot through his words. "A beautiful life is gone."

Anger festered in Siv. This guy was living in la-la land. His and his sister's beautiful life was a fabrication. They were killers with good teeth, nice hair, and a pricey education.

Siv had seen what mattered. The small things. Being kind. Doing the right thing. Treating people with dignity. Looking out for others.

Everything Ryder Morgan stood for.

Enough. She'd had enough. Siv whipped around. Her hit sent the gun flying out of Foster's hand.

He cried out, and she heard shouts and running footsteps.

Her guys were coming.

With a wild cry, Foster threw himself at her. He grabbed her around her thighs and lifted.

Her pulse spiked.

Oh, faen.

Everything happened so fast. Suddenly, her butt was on the railing, Foster was shoving.

Siv tried to grab the railing. She looked over Foster's head, her heart in her throat. The Norcross men were all sprinting forward, but they were too far away.

Her gaze crashed into Ryder's. He was flying toward her, all strength and power, arms pumping.

Then she and Foster tipped backward into the air and off the bridge.

RYDER FELT HIS WORLD IMPLODE. He watched, horror clawing at his throat, as Siv tipped over the railing, Foster following her.

They fell out of sight.

Off the fucking Golden Gate Bridge.

"*Siv*!" Ryder's roar echoed across the bridge.

Arms grabbed him, yanking him to a stop.

"Let me go!" He fought them.

Cam, his face impossibly grim, and a stone-faced Saxon held onto him. Ryder jerked against their grip.

"I said let me go!"

Vander stepped in front of him. His face was blank, but his dark-blue eyes were pissed.

"Let him go," Vander ordered.

Ryder sprinted to the railing. Siv. *Siv.*

No. It couldn't end like this. He'd just found her. He couldn't have failed her too. He couldn't live without her.

He reached the railing and looked down.

The air rushed out of his chest.

Foster and Siv both lay, spread-eagled, on a mesh platform below.

"Fuck!" Ryder yelled.

The others reached him at the railing.

"The suicide barrier," Vander said.

"The city's still installing it," Saxon added. "Because of all the suicides off the bridge."

Foster scrambled away on all fours and leaped onto the nearby work platform suspended under the bridge.

Siv leaped up, the wind tearing at her clothes, and followed. Ryder's heart was in his damn throat as he watched her jump and land on the work platform.

With a shout, Foster charged at her.

Fucking fuck. The platform had no railings; it just held a few boxes of equipment, and stacks of metal and ropes for installing the suicide barrier.

The workers would all wear harnesses to protect them from the fall when they worked on the platform. His pulse pounded in his ears.

Siv had no harness. One wrong push...

Foster and Siv gripped each other, turning in a circle. As the pair fought, they moved frighteningly close to the edge.

"We have to get down there," Ryder growled.

He saw Siv kick Foster. The man slammed into some boxes. He lunged up and shoved her. Siv skidded...way too close to the edge of the platform.

There was no fear or panic on her face. Despite the long fall below, she was as cool as a damn cucumber.

As Foster attacked again, Ryder realized something else. Siv wasn't trying to kill the man. She was trying to subdue him.

Meanwhile, Christian Foster had nothing left to lose.

The sound of a gunshot had Ryder whirling.

Vander had shot the lock off some large toolboxes. He pushed open the lid. There were harnesses and ropes inside.

Vander grabbed one and shoved it at Ryder, then another at Cam. "Suit up and get down there."

They'd all spent time rigged up in helicopters. It didn't take long to work out the harness and slip it on. Saxon helped Ryder tighten it. Rhys helped Cam.

Vander clipped the ropes onto the railing anchor points. "Go!"

Ryder climbed over the railing, suspended in the air for a second. He saw a ladder, gripped it, and started down.

Cam came over the railing right behind him.

Ryder moved fast. The sounds of fighting were getting louder.

"Stand down, Foster," Siv yelled.

Foster just made an angry sound. Ryder glanced over and saw the man swing at Siv.

She ducked.

Foster staggered back and glanced at the equipment. He snatched up a length of metal pipe about the size of a baseball bat.

Oh, hell.

The man swung and Siv jerked to the side.

Ryder's boots hit the metal and he headed across the platform. He raised his Glock.

"Foster, drop the pipe and get down on your knees."

It was like the man didn't even hear Ryder. He swung at Siv again.

She ducked and tried to knock Foster's legs out from under him.

"I'll circle around him from behind," Cam murmured.

Ryder's brother moved around the stacks of boxes and equipment in the center of the platform.

Ryder edged closer. One clear shot was all he needed.

As Foster swung, Siv grabbed the pipe, her arms straining. She and Foster shoved at each other.

Then he wrenched the pipe free.

Siv staggered, throwing her arms up, teetering on the edge of the platform.

Fuck. Ryder fired.

The bullet flew past Foster's ear and the man staggered, slamming sideways into one corner of the platform. He knocked into a crate full of tools. It tipped, teetered, then rammed into the platform support.

There was a groaning sound.

Suddenly, the support gave way, and the platform tilted.

Oh, shit.

Tools, ropes, and metal slid, some of it sliding off and falling like a rain of metal down toward the water of the Bay.

"Siv!" Ryder yelled.

Cool and calm, Siv crouched, gripping the metal flooring.

Foster slid with a scream. He flew off, but managed to grab the edge of the platform, his legs dangling in the air.

"Siv, come this way." Ryder's mouth was dry. One wrong move and Siv would fall.

No. He wasn't losing her. He edged closer.

"I'm slipping." Foster's voice was high-pitched, terrified. "I don't want to die!"

Ryder ignored the man, but Siv was staring at Foster. He saw her snag some rope nearby and tie it to the mesh platform.

There was a look on her face.

Shit. She'd lost a friend like this. This was her own damn nightmare.

"Siv. This way," Ryder urged again.

Cam appeared, moving carefully behind Foster.

"I...can't hold on," Foster sobbed.

Dammit, Ryder wanted to not care. "Cam, can you secure Foster?"

"On it." Cam grabbed a coil of rope, shifting closer.

"Siv?" Ryder asked.

"I'm okay."

Foster made a sound...

Then his fingers slipped off the platform.

"Fuck," Ryder bit out.

Siv sprang up, her left hand gripping the rope.

He realized in a flash what his too-tough, too-honorable woman planned.

His heart dropped into his gut. "Siv!"

She leaped off the platform, sailing out into the air, reaching for Foster.

CHAPTER EIGHTEEN

Siv grabbed Foster's hand. His fingers clung to hers with terrified desperation.

The rope snapped taut, and she took his full weight. Agonizing pain ripped through her shoulder.

"Don't let me go!" he pleaded.

She'd just jumped off a platform to save him. She wasn't about to let him fall to his death.

Foster's legs kicked. The water was a rippling, blue sheet far, far below.

The rope she was holding slipped a little, jolting her. She groaned and the pain made her head spin.

She really wanted to be back on solid ground. And she wanted Ryder. She wanted to tell him that she was falling in love with him.

He hadn't just looked past her tough, prickly exterior, he liked it. He liked her.

"Siv. *Fuck.*" She heard Ryder's voice above her.

She felt a tug on the rope and trusted that he had her.

"Cam, help me," Ryder barked.

Foster's sweaty fingers started to slip through hers. She gritted her teeth and tightened her grip. The pain ripping through her made her stomach contract.

"Don't...move," she said between her teeth.

The rope she was holding slid upward.

Cam reached down and grabbed the back of Foster's shirt. He hauled the man up onto the tilted platform.

She couldn't stop a gasp of pain.

Then she was pulled up and into Ryder's arms.

"I've got you. I've got you." He pressed his face to her hair. His big body shuddered.

She groaned.

"Shit, babe. Your shoulder's dislocated. Come on." He lifted her into his arms.

For once, Siv didn't fight to stand on her own. She leaned into him, closed her eyes, and let him take care of her.

He tried not to jostle her shoulder as he climbed a ladder, his harness being hauled up from above, but each movement sent bolts of agony through her. She bit her lip.

"I'm sorry, babe. We're nearly there."

Finally, they were hauled over the railing. Dimly, she noted sirens in the distance.

Ryder set her down, and went into medic mode as he checked her over.

Nearby, Saxon and Rhys yanked Cam and Foster back onto the bridge.

Vander crouched in front of Siv. "Decided to go for a swing?"

She tried to smile. "Couldn't let him die. I want him to pay. For the world to see what he and his sister did to Robbie and the others."

She felt fingers brush her jaw and looked up into Ryder's face. The look in his eyes stole her breath.

"Thank you, Siv." Another brush of his calloused fingers. "Now, let's sort out this shoulder. I can pop it back in and that'll stop a lot of the pain."

She blew out a shuddering breath. She knew exactly how much this was going to hurt.

She met Vander's gaze.

Her boss pulled a face. "It sucks, I know. I've dislocated my shoulder twice."

"And once, on a mission, he popped it back in himself," Rhys said from nearby.

More proof Vander was badass to the bone.

"On three," Ryder said.

She nodded and braced.

"One—" Ryder manipulated her shoulder with a quick move.

A wave of pain turned her vision white. She cried out, then felt instant relief.

"You asshole, Morgan," she panted.

The men all chuckled.

Ryder kissed the top of her head, sitting down beside her. "God, you have no idea how much I love that snarky tone." He pulled her onto his lap and looked at her. "Or how much I love you."

She sucked in a breath. The unfamiliar sensation of tears forming in her eyes made her blink.

A faint smile curled his lips. "*Jeg elsker deg.*"

"Ryder..."

"I know this is where you're going to tell me you have a ban on men, and we haven't known each other long enough. It's okay, I'll wait. I'll do whatever I have to, in order to make you realize that you're it for me. That I love you and can make you happy."

Siv licked her lips. It was time to take the biggest risk she'd ever taken. "Actually, I was going to tell you that I'm falling in love with you, too."

Ryder's mouth opened and he blinked. He looked stunned.

She grinned.

Around them were more chuckles.

"You're...in love with me?"

She saw wonder and heat dawning in his eyes. She cupped his cheeks, wanting him to realize *just* how much he meant to her. "You're an amazing man, Ryder Morgan. A healer, a protector, a charmer, sexy as hell, and just a good man. And mine."

"Hell, yeah." His mouth took hers. His lips were a little rough, but he was careful not to bump her shoulder.

"Everyone okay? Is Siv all right?"

They broke apart and she looked up. Hunter Morgan, badge on his belt and several police officers behind him, was standing nearby with his hands on his hips.

"Got something for you." Vander hauled Christian Foster up. "One murdering, fraudulent billionaire."

Hunt's gaze darkened. He waved at the officers, who took a subdued Foster toward the police cruiser.

Ryder helped Siv up.

"My woman saved the day," he said, pride clear in his voice.

"It was a team effort," she said. "I just want Foster to get what he deserves."

Hunt nodded. "We have a team at the Foster's estate, as well. I'll need everyone's statements on Caroline Foster's death, and what the hell they were doing with their drug." Hunt glanced at Siv, a wry smile on his rugged face. "And Siv, thanks for not having a high-speed chase, or blowing up the Golden Gate Bridge. If these others were in charge, that's what would've happened."

Vander snorted.

"It was a good idea hiring a woman, Vander." Hunt nodded. "She's adding some restraint and control to your team."

Ryder made a noise. "She just leaped off the bridge, holding a rope, to save Foster's sorry ass."

"Like a damn superhero," Cam said.

Hunt's brows went up. "What?"

Vander clapped a hand to Hunt's arm. "I'm sure Siv will blow something up eventually. Just give her a bit of time."

Siv laughed. "I'll see what I can do."

Ryder rubbed his hand along her lower back. "Now, let's get home, my ass-kicking, Norwegian flower."

THREE DAYS LATER, Siv strode through the Norcross Security warehouse, eating the last of her blueberry bun. She glanced at her cell phone.

On my way.

She tapped in a reply.

See you when you get here.

How's your shoulder?

She rolled her eyes.

You checked it this morning and you know it's fine.

It seemed fine when you were riding me in the shower this morning.

She felt a flush of heat. It had been a very nice way to start the day.

They'd been staying at her place. After the events on the Golden Gate Bridge, Ryder had packed a bag of his stuff and brought it over, along with his bad-tempered cat.

The ornery feline treated Ryder with disdain, but Crank really liked Siv. He was always trying to get into her lap, much to Ryder's annoyance.

Don't be smug. Now get your fine ass over here. You're taking me to lunch.

Coming. So...what are you wearing?

Do you ever not think about sex, Morgan?

Not when it comes to you, my sweet, sexy honningblomst.

She couldn't stop her smile.

"Siv?"

She turned to see Vander.

"I just wanted to let you know that the Foster's story is hitting the press. The whole sordid deal—Trelaskin, the illegal testing, the people who lost their lives. Everything Caroline and Christian Foster have done."

She lifted her chin. "Good." Justice felt damn fine.

"Christian Foster is facing a slew of charges. Chiron's shares have crashed. I managed to keep yours and Ryder's names out of it, but Norcross Security will be mentioned. Oh, and the nurse at the clinic and the assistant medical examiner involved were both charged, as well."

Satisfaction felt *really* good. Robbie and the others finally got justice. Ryder would be so happy. "That's great news."

"Peter Wilcox will be in soon for the final debrief, and wants to meet with you," Vander said.

She nodded.

Her boss gave her a faint smile. "Good work, Siv. It's nice to have you on the team."

As he stalked off, she smiled. Life really was pretty damn good. She had a hot man who loved her. A job she really enjoyed. And colleagues she liked. Their nosy partners were even growing on her.

The ladies of Norcross had descended on her place within hours of the incident on the bridge. They'd brought ice packs, hot packs, drinks, chocolates, and take out. Siv smiled. They were her friends now, whether she liked it or not.

"Siv?"

The male voice made her stiffen and look up. Jeez, she couldn't catch a break.

Johan was walking toward her.

What the hell?

She took him in—gleaming, blond hair, handsome face, lean body, nice clothes. She could see what attracted her to him initially, but looking at him now, he seemed so...bland. He had no presence or sense of self.

"God, Siv, you look great."

Then he shocked her by hugging her.

What the...? She pushed him away.

"Johan, what are you doing here?"

He raked a hand through his hair. "I had time to think, and I realized that I made a big mistake."

She frowned. "About what?"

"Us. I miss you."

Her eyebrows winged up. "And you flew all the way to San Francisco to tell me?"

He smiled. "Yes."

He looked like he thought he deserved praise for that. When she just stared at him, his smiled wavered.

He grabbed her hand. "We had something, Siv, and I took it for granted."

She tried to tug her hand free. "Where's your fiancée?"

"You don't need to worry about her. That was a mistake, too. It's over with Marit. I realized that my heart belongs to you."

God, she felt like she was trapped in a bad movie. "Look, Johan—"

He yanked her close and cupped her cheek. "Siv, I want you back."

Before she could talk, she felt a prickle and looked up.

A thunderous-looking Ryder was heading toward them.

Uh-oh.

He did *not* look happy. His gaze snapped to Johan, and if looks could kill, Johan would be writhing in the corner bleeding.

Siv cleared her throat. "Johan—"

"Step back, asshole." Ryder shoved Johan back.

"Hey." Her ex straightened his shirt. "This is between me and my girlfriend."

Siv blinked. *What?*

Ryder's scowl darkened and he looked at her. "This is the asshole?"

She nodded.

Johan straightened. "I don't know who you are, but we'd like some privacy, please."

Ryder crossed his arms over his chest. "No."

Siv got distracted for a second, looking at his tattoo. Then Johan bristled. He was used to getting his own way.

"She's done with you," Ryder said.

"I don't know who you are, but this is none of your business," Johan said.

"It is my business, because I'm Siv's man."

She watched Johan's brows knit.

"Excuse me?" her ex said.

"It was me she was riding in the shower this morning, my name she was moaning. It's Ryder Morgan, by the way."

Siv stifled a laugh and watched as Johan's mouth dropped open, and he made an inarticulate sound.

She crossed her arms. "Subtle, Morgan."

"Men like him don't understand subtle." Ryder tugged her close and kissed her.

"You wouldn't know subtle if it hit you in the head," she whispered against his lips.

He shot her one of his blinding, sexy smiles.

"Siv, you're...with this man?"

She turned back to Johan. "Yes."

His face hardened. "That was fast."

She narrowed her gaze and made a scoffing sound. "You got *engaged* weeks after we broke up. You cheated on me."

"That was a mistake—"

"No, us being together was a mistake." She took Ryder's hand. "I'm not just with Ryder, I'm in love with him."

His fingers clenched on hers. "*Babe.*"

That look in his eyes, like he'd won the jackpot, arrowed straight to her heart.

"I didn't know what love was before I met Ryder," she said. "I'm right where I'm supposed to be."

Ryder reached out and touched the Viking shield pendant around her neck—the one he'd given her that she now never took off. He kissed her again, and neither of them watched, as Johan strode off in a huff.

A throat clearing made them break apart. Vander stood nearby, a half-smile on his face.

"If you're done, I have Peter Wilcox in my office waiting to talk with you both."

Siv tightened her ponytail and followed her boss. When a hand touched her ass, she smacked it away and gave Ryder a hot look.

In Vander's office, Robbie's brother stood by the window, looking out on the street. He turned.

He looked like he had before, a man in a nice suit with a good haircut and an expensive watch. But the helpless rage and weariness were gone, leaving behind just grief on his face.

"Siv, Mr. Morgan, Vander brought me up to speed on your investigation. I wanted to thank you both." He crossed the room.

Siv shook the man's hand. "I'm glad we found the people responsible for your brother's death. Found justice for him."

Peter nodded. "I'll be attending Christian Foster's trial." The man's voice vibrated with rage. "I'll do everything I can to stand for my brother and the others who died. To be a voice for the victims."

There was a deep thread of determination there. Peter Wilcox wasn't going to let Christian Foster wriggle off, and he'd make sure everyone saw Robbie and the others as real people, not just faceless homeless people no one cared about.

Peter turned to Ryder. "Thomas talked about you, Mr. Morgan. You called him Robbie, right?"

Ryder nodded. "And it's Ryder." The men shook hands.

"He started using that name when he got out of the military, but he'll always be Thomas to me. He respected you."

"Robbie was my friend, and I respected him too. I—" Ryder's voice cracked and he dragged in a breath. "I miss him."

"Me too," Peter said quietly. "His life wasn't what I wanted for him, but I'd long ago accepted I had to be a part of his life, anyway he'd let me. He was a good man."

"He was." Ryder nodded. "He won't be forgotten, by me, or by the people who were his friends. He used to help so many people. Protect them, feed them, help them."

Peter smiled. "That sounds just like Thomas."

"Some of them would like to pay their respects. They're mourning him too. Maybe a memorial or, something?"

"That's a great idea. Can we work together to make that happen?"

Ryder smiled and held out his hand. "Sure thing."

"Thanks, again. Both of you." With a nod at Vander, Peter strode out.

Ryder took Siv's hand. "I'm taking my woman out for lunch."

Vander nodded. "I think she's earned an afternoon off."

Siv huffed. "I just got back to work today."

"You need to take it easy. Ease back into things." Vander waved a hand. "Go."

Ryder dragged her out, picking up speed as they hustled through the warehouse. "Ryder—"

"I have plans, my Norwegian flower. Hot sex at your place, then lunch, and maybe we'll stop at Flour and Branch for dessert."

"Always thinking about sex," she muttered, grinning.

He grinned back. "Yep."

CHAPTER NINETEEN

Ryder stood in front of the small crowd, so many emotions swirling in his chest.

They were in Boeddeker Park, the largest park in the Tenderloin. And the place where Robbie had liked to sit and feed the birds.

Damn, Ryder missed him.

A hand squeezed his fingers. He looked at Siv. It was a cool day, and the sky overhead was filled with gray clouds. She wore a black leather jacket, black pants, and a tan shirt. She was watching him with love and concern in her eyes. He squeezed back.

Peter Wilcox and the rest of the Wilcox family stood nearby. The men of Norcross were behind them, along with Ryder's brothers. Santiago, Iris, and others from the Anderson Clinic were there too. Some were still in their scrubs, having just come from the clinic.

With them was a large group of people who called the streets home, in a wild array of clothes, and woolen hats pulled low over their faces.

Ryder cleared his throat and stepped forward.

"Robbie was my friend. We shared being combat medics in the military, and often swapped stories. We saw some bad shit, so I understood where Robbie came from. He was one of those people with honor and a good heart. I know he helped many of you here, in lots of different ways."

"He made the bad people leave me alone." Annie's high-pitched voice rang across the crowd.

"He gave me food," a man called out.

"He gave me a jacket when I was cold," a young man said.

Ryder saw Peter's face spasm—with sorrow...and pride.

"I will never forget him," Ryder said.

Bish shuffled forward, his hair and beard somewhat tamed for the memorial. He clutched a bunch of flowers in his hands. He cleared his throat nervously. "Robbie was my friend too." Bish's lips trembled. "He was also my family. We stuck together. I was with him when things were good, and when they were not so good." Bish looked at Peter. "He loved his blood family. He talked about you a lot. He was real proud of you."

Peter's lips compressed and he nodded.

"Ryder, Robbie was real proud to call you friend. He told me that you were a classic combat medic. Gold through and through."

Jesus. Ryder didn't want to cry.

Siv slid an arm around him. He tugged her close, thankful for the support, and held on.

"Here's to Robbie." Bish held up the flowers. "The best of us."

Cheers and claps broke out. Someone whistled.

"To Robbie," the crowd yelled.

"To Robbie," Ryder murmured. "Wherever you are, I hope you're at peace, buddy."

Peter stepped forward. He pointed to a van that had just pulled up. Several people in white shirts were climbing out. "I arranged for food and drink. Robbie loved Dan's Kitchen, so I convinced them to deliver. There's plenty for everyone."

There were more cheers.

Both Hunt and Cam came over and hugged Ryder. He saw Siv chatting with Bish and Annie, smiling at the pair.

"Good job, Ryder," Hunt said.

Ryder nodded. "Robbie would've loved this. He'd be sorry he missed the food."

Later, after the memorial had finished, he walked down the sidewalk with Siv.

"I wish I could've met him," she said.

"Robbie would've loved you. He would've threatened to steal you from me."

She smiled and looked ahead. Then she stiffened.

Ryder followed her gaze...

And saw Tattoo Guy and Shaggy Hair smoking on the corner.

Siv straightened, a deadly-looking glint in her eyes.

Uh-oh. "Siv—"

"I'll be right back."

His pulse spiked. "Babe—"

She strode toward the men and Ryder followed.

"Hey!" she called out.

The men's heads whipped around, and their eyes widened.

"Remember me?" she said. "I beat you up. Then you went and got some friends, and jumped my guy."

The two men backed up, like they saw a deadly storm approaching.

Then Siv attacked.

Ryder waited, alert, in case she needed help.

But she didn't.

Her front kick caught Shaggy Hair in the stomach, and he staggered back. She grabbed Tattoo Guy and hammered two quick punches into his gut. Then she swung him around and slammed him into the wall of the closest building.

Next, she grabbed Shaggy's long hair and yanked. He howled. She rammed her knee into his face and sent him to the ground with a pained groan.

Tattoo Guy threw his hands up. "Don't hurt me."

She kicked him again. He landed on top of his friend.

Siv crouched. "You touch my man again, or attack anyone around here, and I'll know. Do you know who I work for?"

The groaning men shook their heads.

"Vander Norcross," she said.

More fear leaked into their eyes.

"I'll be telling him all about you two. Now, make it so I never see your ugly faces again."

They staggered to their feet and hobbled off as quickly as they could.

"Babe," Ryder said as she walked back to him. "I'm as hard as steel right now."

She smiled and grabbed his hand. "Your place is closer than mine."

He yanked her in and kissed her. She bit his lip, hard. Someone else is a little worked up too.

"My place, it is." They set off down the street at a jog.

"YES," Siv breathed.

"Hell, yes, babe," Ryder grunted.

She moved her hips, riding him hard. She loved the way he filled her with every stroke.

It was a few days after the memorial and they were enjoying a lazy Sunday morning. They were still at her place, and Ryder had half moved in.

Siv had discovered that morning sex was the best.

"Fuck me, babe," he muttered.

She pressed her hands to his chest, filling herself with Ryder. His bruises were fading, and she could enjoy every inch of his glorious body anyway she wanted.

He sat up, his arms winding around her, forcing her mouth to his.

Siv kept riding, moving faster and harder. "*Ryder.*" Her breathing was coming in pants.

"Love you, Siv."

"God, I love you, too."

His other hand slid down, toying with her necklace before he went lower, much lower.

"You are magnificent, babe," he murmured. Then his fingers found her clit.

She moaned. "I'm going to come."

"Then come for me."

Siv's back arched and she threw her head back. The pleasure was hot and intense, searing through her. She cried out, her body shaking through her release.

Suddenly, Ryder tossed her on her back. His cock pounded inside her and a second later, he thrust into her, his big body shuddering. His groan was long and loud.

They collapsed on the bed.

"Best way to start the day," he said. "Ever." He pressed a kiss to her mouth. "Now, let's get in the shower. We're meeting Cam, Hunt, and Savannah for a late breakfast remember?"

"Brunch."

"Babe, men don't do brunch."

Siv lifted her head. "It's breakfast, later in the day. That's brunch."

"Nope." He smacked her ass. "Get moving, Pedersen."

They showered. Siv dressed in jeans and a blue knit shirt. She was doing her makeup, while eyeing Ryder in the mirror as he toweled dry. She was lucky she didn't stab herself in the eye with her mascara.

He busted her looking, and posed a little, grinning. That sexy smile... No, it was the total package she loved.

The doorbell rang.

Siv frowned. "I didn't buzz anyone up."

Ryder wrapped a towel around his waist. "I'll get it. You finish up."

She raised her voice. "If it's a woman, please don't have her drooling everywhere." Crank leaped up on the vanity, staring grumpily with his one eye. "Your daddy can't help himself. He charms everyone." She gave the cat a scratch between his ears. Crank purred.

She heard voices. Ryder's deep one, and...a female one.

A familiar female one.

"Oh, *dritt*." She dropped the mascara wand and hustled out.

She found her near-naked lover facing off with her mother.

Christie Pedersen looked like an older, curvier version of Siv. She stayed in good shape with yoga and hiking, and had good genes. She kept her blonde hair dyed shades lighter than Siv's with regular visits to the salon.

Blue eyes sliced to Siv.

"You said no men," her mother clipped. "And here's a handsome one with tattoos, *naked*, in your apartment."

"Hi, Mamma."

"Don't you mamma me. Explain."

Siv cleared her throat. "Well..."

Her mother raised a brow.

"Mrs. Pedersen, it's a real pleasure to meet you." Ryder poured on the charm with a dazzling smile. "You're as beautiful as your daughter. You two could be sisters."

All that did was make her mother's gaze narrow.

Ryder faltered under the glare. "Um..."

Siv snorted "Nice going, Morgan."

"My charm has always worked on everyone, but you," he complained. "And now your mom."

"Apparently Pedersen women are immune," she said.

He closed the distance between them. "Thank God I won you over anyway." He kissed her.

She cupped his jaw. "Because under the bad boy charm is a good man."

Her mother made a sound and Siv jerked. She'd forgotten about her.

Siv straightened. "Mamma—"

Her mom looked between them. "You're in love with him."

Siv's throat tightened. "Yes. I wanted to tell you, but we had a case to close, and it all happened so fast..."

"And you knew I'd object."

"I wanted you to meet him." Ryder slid an arm around Siv. She smiled up at him. "Ryder, this is my mom, Christie. Mom, Ryder Morgan. He's a paramedic."

"And former military," her mom said. "It shows."

"It's nice to meet you," he said. "And just so you know, I'm crazy in love with your daughter."

Siv's mom watched them, then smiled. "I think I believe you."

"Look, we're meeting my brothers for a late breakfast. Will you join us?"

"I'd love to," her mom said.

"I'll..." He waved at his bare chest and towel. "Get dressed." He winked at Siv. "Be right back, my Norwegian flower."

He stalked out and they both watched him go.

"He is very easy to look at," Siv's mom murmured. "That tattoo is fascinating. And his six pack—"

"*Mamma.*"

Her mom walked over and they hugged.

"I'm happy for you, darling."

"I thought you'd be worried," Siv murmured.

"I saw the way you looked at him." Her mom smiled. "And the way he looked at you."

"He makes me happy."

"Good. You deserve that."

Once Ryder was dressed, her mom's suitcases were stored in the guest room, and her mom had stopped to gush over Crank like he was a purebred, they headed to Plow in Potrero Hill. Gia had recommended the farm-to-table restaurant for brunch.

They found Hunt and Savannah, and Cam waiting for them. After introductions, they were seated in the rustic dining room and ordered.

"Savannah, I love art," Siv's mom said. "What a fabulous career."

"Thank you." Savannah pushed a blonde curl back and took a sip of her coffee. "I love it. And since my showing, I've been very busy."

"That showing was where I first saw Siv." Ryder smiled, toying with Siv's hair. "It was love at first sight."

Hunt and Cam snorted, and Savannah laughed, almost spilling her coffee.

Siv's mom blinked. "What?"

"Ryder tried to charm your daughter," Cam said. "Siv laid him out on the dance floor. Flat on his back."

Her mom cupped a hand over her mouth, her eyes dancing.

Ryder sipped his juice. "Like I said, love at first sight."

Suddenly, all the men's cell phones chimed, and Siv's as well.

They all frowned.

Savannah touched Hunt's arm. "Is something wrong?"

Hunt looked at his phone. "Oh, hell."

Siv read the words on her phone.

"Maggie's having the baby," Ryder said.

"That's great," Savannah said.

"Except it sounds like Ace is not coping," Ryder said. "He's in full-blown panic mode."

Siv raised her brows. "The former Red Team hacker, who is as cool as ice providing comms for our missions?"

"I guess it's different when your woman is having your baby," Ryder said.

The men all stood. "They're at Zuckerberg San Francisco General," Hunt said. "That's not far from here."

Siv looked at her mom. "It looks like we need to postpone brunch."

SIV DOZED against Ryder's shoulder, her feet in Cam's lap.

"Want more coffee?" Ryder asked.

She opened her eyes. "What they serve here is *not* coffee."

"Snob."

The waiting room was still full of a good portion of the gang. Maggie's parents and Ace's parents sat chatting to each other. Mr. and Mrs. Norcross had come by for a bit, and the gang had filtered in and out over the last day. Siv's mom was back at the apartment keeping Crank company.

Siv and Ryder had gone home to sleep and had come back this morning.

"God, I didn't know having a baby took this long." Siv felt vaguely horrified. "In the movies, they have a few contractions and the baby pops out."

"You know better than to believe the movies," Ryder said. "You want some?"

She blinked. "Kids?"

He nodded.

Siv shoved off the thought that poor Maggie had been in labor for over twenty-four hours. It was replaced with an image of a grinning, irreverent little boy with his father's green eyes and smile.

"Yeah," she whispered. "One day."

Suddenly, the doors opened. The entire room jerked to attention.

An exhausted Ace appeared, holding a tiny bundle of yellow blankets. "Baby Isabel has arrived." The new father's smile was beaming. "And she's perfect."

"And Maggie?" Vander asked.

"Well, there was some cussing," Ace said.

The crowd laughed.

"But she's great. She was amazing." Ace tilted his arms, showing off his dark-haired baby girl.

Everyone rushed forward, trying to get a look at the baby.

As they waited their turn, Siv saw Cam frowning. Ryder's brother lifted his cell phone to his ear. "Saskia? Are you there?" Then he lowered it and shook his head.

Ryder raised a brow. "Saskia Hawke?"

Siv had heard Savannah mention her best friend in New York. Saskia was a ballet dancer.

She was also the sister of a very dangerous, well-connected man, Killian Hawke. He was the owner of Sentinel Security and had helped out Norcross Security when Savannah was in danger.

Cam shrugged. "We traded numbers when she was in San Francisco. She just called me, said my name, and then the call cut off." He thumbed the screen and shook his head. "I tried to call her back, but it won't connect."

"I'm sure she's fine," Siv said. "Maybe Vander could contact Killian?"

Cam nodded, but his frown didn't go away. "I'm going to take off. Tell Ace congrats from me. I'll catch you guys later."

Ace appeared with the baby.

"I want to hold her." Ryder took the baby with practiced ease.

Holy hormones. There was something about a hot guy cradling a baby with his inked, muscular arm. Siv felt all kinds of butterflies take flight in her belly.

Ryder caught her gaze and winked.

Yes, this man made her happy. He'd be her rock, her support, her lover, her strength, *hers*. For always.

She leaned into him, one hand stroking the baby's soft hair. One day, if they were blessed, he'd cradle their baby in his arms. And they'd love each other more every day.

Making a new start was the best thing she'd ever done.

No, letting Ryder Morgan charm his way into her heart was the best thing she'd ever done.

I hope you enjoyed Siv and Ryder's story!

Norcross Security continues with *The Protector*, starring the final Morgan brother, Camden, coming in June 2022.

For more action romance (and some more cameos by Killian Hawke and Vander Norcross), check out the first book in the **Billionaire Heists trilogy**, *Stealing from Mr. Rich* (Zane Roth's story). **Read on for a preview of the first chapter.**

Don't miss out! For updates about new releases, free books, and other fun stuff, sign up for my VIP mailing list and get your *free box set* containing three action-packed romances.

Visit here to get started: www.annahackett.com

Would you like
a FREE BOX SET
of my books?

PREVIEW: STEALING FROM MR. RICH

Monroe

The old-fashioned Rosengrens safe was a beauty.

I carefully turned the combination dial, then pressed closer to the safe. The metal was cool under my fingertips. The safe wasn't pretty, but stout and secure. There was something to be said for solid security.

Rosengrens had started making safes in Sweden over a hundred years ago. They were good at it. I listened to the pins, waiting for contact. Newer safes had internals made from lightweight materials to reduce sensory feedback, so I didn't get to use these skills very often.

Some people could play the piano, I could play a safe. The tiny vibration I was waiting for reached my fingertips, followed by the faintest click.

"I've gotcha, old girl." The Rosengrens had quite a few quirks, but my blood sang as I moved the dial again.

I heard a louder click and spun the handle.

The safe door swung open. Inside, I saw stacks of jewelry cases and wads of hundred-dollar bills. *Nice.*

Standing, I dusted my hands off on my jeans. "There you go, Mr. Goldstein."

"You are a doll, Monroe O'Connor. Thank you."

The older man, dressed neatly in pressed chinos and a blue shirt, grinned at me. He had coke-bottle glasses, wispy, white hair, and a wrinkled face.

I smiled at him. Mr. Goldstein was one of my favorite people. "I'll send you my bill."

His grin widened. "I don't know what I'd do without you."

I raised a brow. "You could stop forgetting your safe combination."

The wealthy old man called me every month or so to open his safe. Right now, we were standing in the home office of his expensive Park Avenue penthouse.

It was decorated in what I thought of as "rich, old man." There were heavy drapes, gold-framed artwork, lots of dark wood—including the built-in shelves around the safe—and a huge desk.

"Then I wouldn't get to see your pretty face," he said.

I smiled and patted his shoulder. "I'll see you next month, Mr. Goldstein." The poor man was lonely. His wife had died the year before, and his only son lived in Europe.

"Sure thing, Monroe. I'll have some of those donuts you like."

We headed for the front door and my chest tightened. I understood feeling lonely. "You could do with some new locks on your door. I mean, your building has top-notch security, but you can never be too careful. Pop by the shop if you want to talk locks."

He beamed at me and held the door open. "I might do that."

"Bye, Mr. Goldstein."

I headed down the plush hall to the elevator. Everything in the building screamed old money. I felt like an imposter just being in the building. Like I had "daughter of a criminal" stamped on my head.

Pulling out my cell phone, I pulled up my accounting app and entered Mr. Goldstein's callout. Next, I checked my messages.

Still nothing from Maguire.

Frowning, I bit my lip. That made it three days since I'd heard from my little brother. I shot him off a quick text.

"Text me back, Mag," I muttered.

The elevator opened and I stepped in, trying not to

worry about Maguire. He was an adult, but I'd practically raised him. Most days it felt like I had a twenty-four-year-old kid.

The elevator slowed and stopped at another floor. An older, well-dressed couple entered. They eyed me and my well-worn jeans like I'd crawled out from under a rock.

I smiled. "Good morning."

Yeah, yeah, I'm not wearing designer duds, and my bank account doesn't have a gazillion zeros. You're so much better than me.

Ignoring them, I scrolled through Instagram. When we finally reached the lobby, the couple shot me another dubious look before they left. I strode out across the marble-lined space and rolled my eyes.

During my teens, I'd cared about what people thought. Everyone had known that my father was Terry O'Connor—expert thief, safecracker, and con man. I'd felt every repulsed look and sly smirk at high school.

Then I'd grown up, cultivated some thicker skin, and learned not to care. *Fuck 'em.* People who looked down on others for things outside their control were assholes.

I wrinkled my nose. Okay, it was easier said than done.

When I walked outside, the street was busy. I smiled, breathing in the scent of New York—car exhaust, burnt meat, and rotting trash. Besides, most people cared more about themselves. They judged you, left you bleeding, then forgot you in the blink of an eye.

I unlocked my bicycle, and pulled on my helmet,

then set off down the street. I needed to get to the store. The ride wasn't long, but I spent every second worrying about Mag.

My brother had a knack for finding trouble. I sighed. After a childhood, where both our mothers had taken off, and Da was in and out of jail, Mag was entitled to being a bit messed up. The O'Connors were a long way from the Brady Bunch.

I pulled up in front of my shop in Hell's Kitchen and stopped for a second.

I grinned. *All mine.*

Okay, I didn't own the building, but I owned the store. The sign above the shop said *Lady Locksmith.* The logo was lipstick red—a woman's hand with gorgeous red nails, holding a set of keys.

After I locked up my bike, I strode inside. A chime sounded.

God, I loved the place. It was filled with glossy, warm-wood shelves lined with displays of state-of-the-art locks and safes. A key-cutting machine sat at the back.

A blonde head popped up from behind a long, shiny counter.

"You're back," Sabrina said.

My best friend looked like a doll—small, petite, with a head of golden curls.

We'd met doing our business degrees at college, and had become fast friends. Sabrina had always wanted to be tall and sexy, but had to settle for small and cute. She was my manager, and was getting married in a month.

"Yeah, Mr. Goldstein forgot his safe code again," I said.

Sabrina snorted. "That old coot doesn't forget, he just likes looking at your ass."

"He's harmless. He's nice, and lonely. How's the team doing?"

Sabrina leaned forward, pulling out her tablet. I often wondered if she slept with it. "Liz is out back unpacking stock." Sabrina's nose wrinkled. "McRoberts overcharged us on the Schlage locks again."

"That prick." He was always trying to screw me over. "I'll call him."

"Paola, Kat, and Isabella are all out on jobs."

Excellent. Business was doing well. Lady Locksmith specialized in providing female locksmiths to all the single ladies of New York. They also advised on how to keep them safe—securing locks, doors, and windows.

I had a dream of one day seeing multiple Lady Locksmiths around the city. Hell, around every city. A girl could dream. Growing up, once I understood the damage my father did to other people, all I'd wanted was to be respectable. To earn my own way and add to the world, not take from it.

"Did you get that new article I sent you to post on the blog?" I asked.

Sabrina nodded. "It'll go live shortly, and then I'll post on Insta, as well."

When I had the time, I wrote articles on how women—single *and* married—should secure their homes. My latest was aimed at domestic-violence survivors, and helping them feel safe. I donated my time to Nightingale House, a local shelter that helped women leaving DV situations, and I installed locks for them, free of charge.

"We should start a podcast," Sabrina said.

I wrinkled my nose. "I don't have time to sit around recording stuff." I did my fair share of callouts for jobs, plus at night I had to stay on top of the business-side of the store.

"Fine, fine." Sabrina leaned against the counter and eyed my jeans. "Damn, I hate you for being tall, long, and gorgeous. You're going to look *way* too beautiful as my maid of honor." She waved a hand between us. "You're all tall, sleek, and dark-haired, and I'm...the opposite."

I had some distant Black Irish ancestor to thank for my pale skin and ink-black hair. Growing up, I wanted to be short, blonde, and tanned. I snorted. "Beauty comes in all different forms, Sabrina." I gripped her shoulders. "You are so damn pretty, and your fiancé happens to think you are the most beautiful woman in the world. Andrew is gaga over you."

Sabrina sighed happily. "He does and he is." A pause. "So, do you have a date for my wedding yet?" My bestie's voice turned breezy and casual.

Uh-oh. I froze. All the wedding prep had sent my normally easygoing best friend a bit crazy. And I knew very well not to trust that tone.

I edged toward my office. "Not yet."

Sabrina's blue eyes sparked. "It's only *four* weeks away, Monroe. The maid of honor can't come alone."

"I'll be busy helping you out—"

"Find a date, Monroe."

"I don't want to just pick anyone for your wedding—"

Sabrina stomped her foot. "Find someone, or I'll find someone for you."

I held up my hands. "Okay, okay." I headed for my office. "I'll—" My cell phone rang. *Yes*. "I've got a call. Got to go." I dove through the office door.

"I won't forget," Sabrina yelled. "I'll revoke your best-friend status, if I have to."

I closed the door on my bridezilla bestie and looked at the phone.

Maguire. Finally.

I stabbed the call button. "Where have you been?"

"We have your brother," a robotic voice said.

My blood ran cold. My chest felt like it had filled with concrete.

"If you want to keep him alive, you'll do exactly as I say."

Zane

God, this party was boring.

Zane Roth sipped his wine and glanced around the ballroom at the Mandarin Oriental. The party held the Who's Who of New York society, all dressed up in their glittering best. The ceiling shimmered with a sea of crystal lights, tall flower arrangements dominated the tables, and the wall of windows had a great view of the Manhattan skyline.

Everything was picture perfect...and boring.

If it wasn't for the charity auction, he wouldn't be dressed in his tuxedo and dodging annoying people.

"I'm so sick of these parties," he muttered.

A snort came from beside him.

One of his best friends, Maverick Rivera, sipped his wine. "You were voted New York's sexiest billionaire bachelor. You should be loving this shindig."

Mav had been one of his best friends since college. Like Zane, Maverick hadn't come from wealth. They'd both earned it the old-fashioned way. Zane loved numbers and money, and had made Wall Street his hunting ground. Mav was a geek, despite not looking like a stereotypical one. He'd grown up in a strong, Mexican-American family, and with his brown skin, broad shoulders, and the fact that he worked out a lot, no one would pick him for a tech billionaire.

But under the big body, the man was a computer geek to the bone.

"All the society mamas are giving you lots of speculative looks." Mav gave him a small grin.

"Shut it, Rivera."

"They're all dreaming of marrying their daughters off to billionaire Zane Roth, the finance King of Wall Street."

Zane glared. "You done?"

"Oh, I could go on."

"I seem to recall another article about the billionaire bachelors. All three of us." Zane tipped his glass at his friend. "They'll be coming for you, next."

Mav's smile dissolved, and he shrugged a broad shoulder. "I'll toss Kensington at them. He's pretty."

Liam Kensington was the third member of their trio. Unlike Zane and Mav, Liam had come from money, although he worked hard to avoid his bloodsucking family.

Zane saw a woman in a slinky, blue dress shoot him a welcoming smile.

He looked away.

When he'd made his first billion, he'd welcomed the attention. Especially the female attention. He'd bedded more than his fair share of gorgeous women.

Of late, nothing and no one caught his interest. Women all left him feeling numb.

Work. He thrived on that.

A part of him figured he'd never find a woman who made him feel the same way as his work.

"Speak of the devil," Mav said.

Zane looked up to see Liam Kensington striding toward them. With the lean body of a swimmer, clad in a perfectly tailored tuxedo, he looked every inch the billionaire. His gold hair complemented a face the ladies oohed over.

People tried to get his attention, but the real estate mogul ignored everyone.

He reached Zane and Mav, grabbed Zane's wine, and emptied it in two gulps.

"I hate this party. When can we leave?" Having spent his formative years in London, he had a posh British accent. Another thing the ladies loved. "I have a contract to work on, my fundraiser ball to plan, and things to catch up on after our trip to San Francisco."

The three of them had just returned from a business trip to the West Coast.

"Can't leave until the auction's done," Zane said.

Liam sighed. His handsome face often had him voted the best-looking billionaire bachelor.

"Buy up big," Zane said. "Proceeds go to the Boys and Girls Clubs."

"One of your pet charities," Liam said.

"Yeah." Zane's father had left when he was seven. His mom had worked hard to support them. She was his hero. He liked to give back to charities that supported kids growing up in tough circumstances.

He'd set his mom up in a gorgeous house Upstate that she loved. And he was here for her tonight.

"Don't bid on the Phillips-Morley necklace, though," he added. "It's mine."

The necklace had a huge, rectangular sapphire pendant surrounded by diamonds. It was the real-life necklace said to have inspired the necklace in the movie, *Titanic*. It had been given to a young woman, Kate Florence Phillips, by her lover, Henry Samuel Morley. The two had run away together and booked passage on the Titanic.

Unfortunately for poor Kate, Henry had drowned when the ship had sunk. She'd returned to England with the necklace and a baby in her belly.

Zane's mother had always loved the story and pored over pictures of the necklace. She'd told him the story of the lovers, over and over.

"It was a gift from a man to a woman he loved. She was a shop girl, and he owned the store, but they fell in love, even though society frowned on their love." She sighed. "That's true love, Zane. Devotion, loyalty, through the good times and the bad."

Everything Carol Roth had never known.

Of course, it turned out old Henry was much older than his lover, and already married. But Zane didn't want to ruin the fairy tale for his mom.

Now, the Phillips-Morley necklace had turned up, and was being offered at auction. And Zane was going to get it for his mom. It was her birthday in a few months.

"Hey, is your fancy, new safe ready yet?" Zane asked Mav.

His friend nodded. "You're getting one of the first ones. I can have my team install it this week."

"Perfect." Mav's new Riv3000 was the latest in high-tech safes and said to be unbreakable. "I'll keep the necklace in it until my mom's birthday."

Someone called out Liam's name. With a sigh, their friend forced a smile. "Can't dodge this one. Simpson's an investor in my Brooklyn project. I'll be back."

"Need a refill?" Zane asked Mav.

"Sure."

Zane headed for the bar. He'd almost reached it when a manicured hand snagged his arm.

"Zane."

He looked down at the woman and barely swallowed his groan. "Allegra. You look lovely this evening."

She did. Allegra Montgomery's shimmery, silver dress hugged her slender figure, and her cloud of mahogany brown hair accented her beautiful face. As the only daughter of a wealthy New York family—her father was from *the* Montgomery family and her mother was a former Miss America—Allegra was well-bred and well-educated but also, as he'd discovered, spoiled and liked getting her way.

Her dark eyes bored into him. "I'm sorry things ended badly for us the other month. I was..." Her voice lowered, and she stroked his forearm. "I miss you. I was hoping we could catch up again."

Zane arched a brow. They'd dated for a few weeks, shared a few dinners, and some decent sex. But Allegra liked being the center of attention, complained that he worked too much, and had constantly hounded him to take her on vacation. Preferably on a private jet to Tahiti or the Maldives.

When she'd asked him if it would be too much for him to give her a credit card of her own, for monthly expenses, Zane had exited stage left.

"I don't think so, Allegra. We aren't...compatible."

Her full lips turned into a pout. "I thought we were *very* compatible."

He cleared his throat. "I heard you moved on. With Chip Huffington."

Allegra waved a hand. "Oh, that's nothing serious."

And Chip was only a millionaire. Allegra would see that as a step down. In fact, Zane felt like every time she looked at him, he could almost see little dollar signs in her eyes.

He dredged up a smile. "I wish you all the best, Allegra. Good evening." He sidestepped her and made a beeline for the bar.

"What can I get you?" the bartender asked.

Wine wasn't going to cut it. It would probably be frowned on to ask for an entire bottle of Scotch. "Two glasses of Scotch, please. On the rocks. Do you have Macallan?"

"No, sorry, sir. Will Glenfiddich do?"

"Sure."

"Ladies and gentlemen," a voice said over the loudspeaker. The lights lowered. "I hope you're ready to spend big for a wonderful cause."

Carrying the drinks, Zane hurried back to Mav and Liam. He handed Mav a glass.

"Let's do this," Mav grumbled. "And next time, I'll make a generous online donation so I don't have to come to the party."

"Drinks at my place after I get the necklace," Zane said. "I have a very good bottle of Macallan."

Mav stilled. "How good?"

"Macallan 25. Single malt."

"I'm there," Liam said.

Mav lifted his chin.

Ahead, Zane watched the evening's host lift a black cloth off a pedestal. He stared at the necklace, the sapphire glittering under the lights.

There it was.

The sapphire was a deep, rich blue. Just like all the photos his mother had shown him.

"Get that damn necklace, Roth, and let's get out of here," Mav said.

Zane nodded. He'd get the necklace for the one woman in his life who rarely asked for anything, then escape the rest of the bloodsuckers and hang with his friends.

Billionaire Heists

Stealing from Mr. Rich
Blackmailing Mr. Bossman
Hacking Mr. CEO

PREVIEW: TEAM 52 AND THS

Want to learn more about the mysterious, covert *Team 52*? Check out the first book in the series, *Mission: Her Protection.*

When Rowan's Arctic research team pulls a strange object out of the ice in Northern

Canada, things start to go wrong...very, very wrong. Rescued by a covert, black ops team, she finds herself in the powerful arms of a man with scary gold eyes. A man who vows to do everything and anything to protect her...

Dr. Rowan Schafer has learned it's best to do things herself and not depend on anyone else. Her cold, academic parents taught her that lesson. She loves the challenge of running a research base, until the day her scientists discover the object in a retreating glacier. Under attack, Rowan finds herself fighting to survive... until the mysterious Team 52 arrives.

Former special forces Marine Lachlan Hunter's military career ended in blood and screams, until he was recruited to lead a special team. A team tasked with a top-secret mission—to secure and safeguard pieces of powerful ancient technology. Married to his job, he's done too much and seen too much to risk inflicting his demons on a woman. But when his team arrives in the Arctic, he uncovers both an unexplained artifact, and a young girl from his past, now all grown up. A woman who ignites emotions inside him like never before.

But as Team 52 heads back to their base in Nevada, other hostile forces are after the artifact. Rowan finds herself under attack, and as the bullets fly, Lachlan vows to protect her at all costs. But in the face of danger like they've never seen before, will it be enough to keep her alive.

Team 52
Mission: Her Protection
Mission: Her Rescue
Mission: Her Security
Mission: Her Defense
Mission: Her Safety
Mission: Her Freedom
Mission: Her Shield
Also Available as Audiobooks!

Want to learn more about *Treasure Hunter Security*? Check out the first book in the series, *Undiscovered*, Declan Ward's action-packed story.

One former Navy SEAL. One dedicated archeologist. One secret map to a fabulous lost oasis.

Finding undiscovered treasures is always daring, dangerous, and deadly. Perfect for the men of Treasure Hunter Security. Former Navy SEAL Declan Ward is haunted by the demons of his past and throws everything he has into his security business—Treasure Hunter Security. Dangerous archeological digs – no problem. Daring expeditions – sure thing. Museum security for invaluable exhibits – easy. But on a simple dig in the Egyptian desert, he collides with a stubborn, smart archeologist, Dr. Layne Rush, and together they get swept into a deadly treasure hunt for a mythical lost oasis. When an evil from his past reappears, Declan vows to do anything to protect Layne.

Dr. Layne Rush is dedicated to building a successful career—a promise to the parents she lost far too young. But when her dig is plagued by strange accidents, targeted by a lethal black market antiquities ring, and artifacts are stolen, she is forced to turn to Treasure Hunter Security, and to the tough, sexy, and too-used-to-giving-orders Declan. Soon her organized dig morphs into a wild treasure hunt across the desert dunes.

Danger is hunting them every step of the way, and Layne and Declan must find a way to work together...to not only find the treasure but to survive.

Treasure Hunter Security

Undiscovered

Uncharted

Unexplored

Unfathomed

Untraveled
Unmapped
Unidentified
Undetected
Also Available as Audiobooks!

ALSO BY ANNA HACKETT

Norcross Security

The Investigator

The Troubleshooter

The Specialist

The Bodyguard

The Hacker

The Powerbroker

The Detective

The Medic

Billionaire Heists

Stealing from Mr. Rich

Blackmailing Mr. Bossman

Hacking Mr. CEO

Team 52

Mission: Her Protection

Mission: Her Rescue

Mission: Her Security

Mission: Her Defense

Mission: Her Safety

Mission: Her Freedom

Mission: Her Shield

Mission: Her Justice

Also Available as Audiobooks!

Treasure Hunter Security

Undiscovered

Uncharted

Unexplored

Unfathomed

Untraveled

Unmapped

Unidentified

Undetected

Also Available as Audiobooks!

Galactic Kings

Overlord

Emperor

Eon Warriors

Edge of Eon

Touch of Eon

Heart of Eon

Kiss of Eon

Mark of Eon

Claim of Eon

Storm of Eon

Soul of Eon

King of Eon

Also Available as Audiobooks!

Galactic Gladiators: House of Rone

Sentinel

Defender

Centurion

Paladin

Guard

Weapons Master

Also Available as Audiobooks!

Galactic Gladiators

Gladiator

Warrior

Hero

Protector

Champion

Barbarian

Beast

Rogue

Guardian

Cyborg

Imperator

Hunter

Also Available as Audiobooks!

Hell Squad

Marcus

Cruz

Gabe

Reed

Roth

Noah

Shaw

Holmes

Niko

Finn

Devlin

Theron

Hemi

Ash

Levi

Manu

Griff

Dom

Survivors

Tane

Also Available as Audiobooks!

The Anomaly Series

Time Thief

Mind Raider

Soul Stealer

Salvation

Anomaly Series Box Set

The Phoenix Adventures

Among Galactic Ruins

At Star's End

In the Devil's Nebula

On a Rogue Planet

Beneath a Trojan Moon

Beyond Galaxy's Edge

On a Cyborg Planet

Return to Dark Earth

On a Barbarian World

Lost in Barbarian Space

Through Uncharted Space

Crashed on an Ice World

Perma Series

Winter Fusion

A Galactic Holiday

Warriors of the Wind

Tempest

Storm & Seduction

Fury & Darkness

Standalone Titles

Savage Dragon

Hunter's Surrender

One Night with the Wolf

For more information visit www.annahackett.com

ABOUT THE AUTHOR

I'm a USA Today bestselling romance author who's passionate about ***fast-paced, emotion-filled*** contemporary romantic suspense and science fiction romance. I love writing about people overcoming unbeatable odds and achieving seemingly impossible goals. I like to believe it's possible for all of us to do the same.

I live in Australia with my own personal hero and two very busy, always-on-the-move sons.

For release dates, behind-the-scenes info, free books, and other fun stuff, sign up for the latest news here:

Website: www.annahackett.com

Made in the USA
Coppell, TX
30 April 2025

48862597R00166